Esther

ELLEN GUNDERSON
TRAYLOR

HARVEST HOUSE PUBLISHERS
Eugene, Oregon 97402

Other Books by
Ellen Gunderson Traylor

Song of Abraham
John—Son of Thunder
Mary Magdalene   *
Noah
Ruth—A Love Story
Jonah
Mark
Joseph
Moses
Joshua
Samson

ESTHER

Copyright © 1994 by Harvest House Publishers
Eugene, Oregon 97402

Library of Congress Catalog Card Number 87-081246
ISBN 1-56507-272-3

Printed in the United States of America.

97 98 99 00 01 — 10 9 8 7 6 5 4 3

To Eric,
who loved beauty.

Contents

A Note to the Reader

Thy lovingkindness, O LORD,
extends to the heavens,
Thy faithfulness reaches to the skies.
The righteousness is like
the mountains of God;
Thy judgments are like a great deep.

Psalm 36:5,6 NASB

A Note to the Reader

In a tiny hall of the Oriental Institute Museum, on the campus of the University of Chicago, there is an enormous artifact—the 20,000-pound black stone head of a guardian bull. Transplanted from the grounds of Persepolis, the ancient Persian ceremonial capital, this cold creature stares down upon tourists and scholars with centuries-old aloofness. Could it speak, it would doubtless tell fabulous tales of the grand empire which once ruled half the world.

Having embroiled myself in the study of Esther, the biblical queen who was for a time first lady of that empire, I was overcome with feeling when I first set eyes upon this heartless creature. Esther herself, fairest woman on earth and pure of heart in devotion to her Jewish heritage, had most likely passed before this very statue, and the sightless rock had glowered down on her, just as it now did on me.

In an instant, I sensed a personal link with the young girl whom I had studied, understanding for the first time how frightened she must have been when carried away to become wife of the despot, Xerxes.

Esther's name does not show up in any secular chronicle. Herodotus, the most meticulous recorder of Xerxes' life and of the Greek-Persian Wars, mentions Amestris (probably the biblical Vashti), who was the rightful queen. Only the Bible tells of Hadassah, the orphaned Jewess who rose to the throne, unhappily taking on a pagan name and filling the place where the first noble lady should have remained.

Although overlooked by secular historians, the tale of Esther is crucial to the story of Israel. For Esther was a savior to her people, raised for a purpose higher than worldly acclaim.

"What was she like?" I would have asked the great bull, if I could. "When you and your brothers in Persepolis and Susa loomed above her, did she tremble?"

Only a novelist's imagination could assist me toward the answer. The Scriptures, though telling us all we know of this obscure queen, are typically scant in revealing the heroine's heart. We see the plot, but must interpret the character's motivations and emotions with the aid of prayer and intuition alone. This is true not only for Esther, but for Vashti, Xerxes, and the host of other people who fill the pages of God's Word.

Fumbling as our reconstruction may be, we will not go far wrong if we remember that these were folk of flesh and blood, who once loved and cried and laughed. And that they, like we, were guided through their steps by the Sovereign God who rules all history and governs each life for his ultimate purpose.

If we can apply this principle as we read of those who lived so long ago, we also can apply it to ourselves. No one's circumstances, no matter how mysterious or confounding, are outside God's grand design. Our Father knows the end from the beginning. Despite our frustrated attempts to understand, he will always be proven the Master Architect of all things.

May you find encouragement for your hard times and the laughter of the Lord in all your triumphs.

—Ellen Traylor

ESTHER

PART I
The King and the Prince

1

Purple dusk had settled over Persia's western desert. A rush of cool wind swept through Susa on its way to the Gulf, bearing the scent of lilies across the housetops.

It was Spring. Tomorrow would begin a new imperial year.

Amestris Vashti, daughter of Otanes, shivered and glanced south toward Persepolis, the distant ceremonial capital, where the revelry of New Year's Eve would be even more boisterous than in this northern citadel.

Vashti's private balcony afforded an expansive view across Susa's southern wall, and in this sanctum of her father's home she was free for a moment from the din in the streets beyond the river.

One of the mansions of the seven noblest families in Persia, the house of her childhood stood safely tucked atop Susa's acropolis. Rarely had Vashti found it necessary to mingle with the commoners who lived in the shadow of the royal mount, but New Year's Eve required it.

Vashti, along with her royal sisters (girls born to the highest homes in the land), had ridden through town this day in open carriages, bearing long-stemmed lilies in their hands and wearing pink irises in their hair. Though they had been cheered and praised by adoring masses, Vashti had not enjoyed it.

She would have preferred to accompany her cousins, the young princes of King Darius, to Persepolis.

But that journey was for boys alone.

Pushing slender fingers through a tousle of long black curls, she lifted her face to the wind and let the cool air spill over her bare arms. As she wrapped her fringed shawl about her shoulders, she remembered that Prince Xerxes had once stood with her upon this very balcony.

They had been mere children and very innocent. But when the chamberlain had found them, he had rebuked them soundly. "It is dark, and you are alone!" he had glowered. "This is indiscretion!"

At the time, being but a young girl, she had not known what "indiscretion" meant. It must be something dreadful, she deduced, and so did Xerxes when they spoke of it in the garden the next day.

That had been a decade ago. Vashti was 16 now, and most of her training for the past ten years had been concerned with discretion and indiscretion. She had come to love being a lady and behaving the part.

And she had come to love Xerxes too, if indeed she had ever *not* loved him.

In truth, she could not remember ever feeling neutral toward the third son of Darius. And she could not recall ever feeling anything for him but admiration.

Certainly her circle of childhood playmates and adolescent companions had been carefully chosen. She had known only a few boys in her growing-up years—sons of nobility and sons of Darius. Well before she had reached puberty, she had been limited in socializing even with these.

But Xerxes had won her heart before she knew she could give it. And being rarely allowed to see him had only bound her to him more surely.

Closing her eyes, she leaned against a fluted column of her lofty porch and tried to envision what he might be doing just now. In a few hours it would be midnight, the first day of the new year, and twelve years since Xerxes' ascension to the office of viceroy. He was 18 now, but he had stood behind his father's throne since he was less than half that old.

Though he was not the monarch's eldest son, he was the first since his coronation. Hence he would one day succeed to the throne.

And should all go as planned, Vashti would be queen.

At midnight in Persepolis the sacred dice would be cast, the "purim," which would determine the appointed dates of special events for the empire's coming year.

"The priests, when they cast the dice, will speak of you and me," the prince had promised her. "On New Year's Eve they will decide our wedding day."

It was fully possible that a quirk of the dice or an interpretation of accompanying omens could throw the date into a later year. But Vashti and Xerxes had prayed to Ahura-Mazda and had taken a second drink from the cup of haoma, pleading that no such delay would take place.

Rarely since their earliest days of childish play had the prince been alone with Vashti. As a small boy and girl they had touched often, had held hands, and had skipped through the mammoth hallways of Susa's palace.

But their encounters were more guarded now. Those fleeting occasions when the prince had brushed her arm in passing or had touched her fingertips at a banquet table were stored in her memory like hallowed gems.

Bronze-skinned and tall, he was a striking figure now—a man and not a boy. Were he to bend over her with his strong neck and able arms, she would tremble, she knew. For she had done so this very morning, when in a stolen moment he had kissed her.

Had that been indiscretion? The chamberlain would have said so. But Vashti was Xerxes' betrothed, his soon-to-be-wife. No one could have kept him from seeking her in the garden and pressing his promises to her.

Vashti opened her eyes. The din in the streets was clearly audible now, even at this far side of the mount. Below wound the Shapur River through the center of town, and beyond the city wall stretched the night-cold desert.

Small strings of light here and there along the sandy expanse marked feudal villages, where proud farmers and craftsmen derived a tolerable living from the irrigated soil. Though Susa was dominated by Persians, every nationality in the empire, from Indian to Ethiopian, composed its population and its suburbs. Tonight the people were free to come and go through the city's open gates, and a constant line of traffic traced the highway between the citadel and the nearby Gulf.

Vashti had often tried to comprehend the enormity of Darius' realm. Susa was only a small fraction of the whole, of the dominions which stretched over three thousand miles across the world and which included 127 provinces from India to Africa.

All this would one day belong to Xerxes. The greatest names on earth, from Babylon to Egypt, bowed the knee to Persia.

And if Darius had his way, even Greece would eventually succumb.

Greece, alone of all civilized nations, had managed to resist tribute to Darius. Its native tongue had not yielded to the Aramaic language. Even Xerxes, properly known as Ahasuerus, was called by the more popular Greek variation.

One day, Darius was determined, he would usurp Grecian hold over southern Europe. He would bring away captive Greek slaves, just as his Babylonian predecessor, Nebuchadnezzar, had done with the Israelites.

But that was *Darius'* plan. *Vashti's* was to marry Xerxes. This was all she cared for.

She would have closed her eyes again, to contemplate him, had her gaze not been caught by certain pedestrians along the desert highway.

Hundreds came and went upon the road, all in festive mood, singing, dancing, reeling from drink.

But the little group which caught her attention was strangely huddled, bent about an elderly man and the bundle he carried in his arms. A couple and a younger fellow walked with the old one, intent on helping him along and watching the little parcel with care.

"Peculiar," Vashti thought; "always they are peculiar."

She had recognized them immediately as Jews, and designated them strange not only because of their dress but because of their typically somber attitude.

Though all Persia partied tonight, these folk, like many of their race, kept to themselves, observing the holiday independently and quietly.

These, of all the folk in Persia's realm, were hardest for her to understand. She neither loved nor hated them, but found them curious oddities.

Were she at hand, she might have asked them why they behaved so strangely, and what was concealed in the wrapper.

But when they disappeared through the city gate she forgot them, and her eyes grew heavy with the dark.

Turning for her chamber, she slipped to bed and hoped the midnight cacophony would not rouse her.

She wished to dream of Xerxes.

2

When the little band of Jews entered the city, they did not turn toward the center of common festivity, the marketplace, but instead crossed the elegant bridge leading toward the acropolis.

Along the foot of the mount stood fine homes amid imperial office buildings and treasuries. These houses and apartments were not so elaborate as those of the Persian nobility but were more handsome than the box-shaped residences of the lower class. These fine homes spoke of success and upward mobility. If a Jew lived in Susa, it was not unlikely that he would live here.

The close-knit folk whom Vashti had observed from her balcony traversed several broad avenues fronting such abodes. The youngest of the group, a slender fellow with smooth features and well-trimmed beard, seemed most anxious to move along but was hindered by the eldest, who was not so spry as he.

"We are almost there, Uncle," the young man spurred him. "Just around the next corner."

"You have done well for yourself, Mordecai," the elder observed, studying his surroundings with proud eyes. "To dwell in a foreign land in finery—that is a task for a Jew. And you have accomplished it!"

The idea of Persia being a "foreign" place, after more than two centuries of his ancestors' residing here, had always struck Mordecai as strange. But he nodded graciously, having heard such assessments all his life.

True, the ancestral Israelites had not come to Mesopotamia willingly. They had been taken captive by Nebuchadnezzar 200 years before—"exiled," as they put it, by the hand of God. But Cyrus the Great had emancipated them. There were no longer Jewish slaves in Babylon or any part of Persia. They had been free to return to Israel, just as all captive people of the realm had been free to return to their homelands.

Since then, of course, other slaves had been taken by Cyrus' successors—but never again the Israelites. The many Jews who had chosen to remain in Persia were free to pursue all the empire had to offer, and they, being industrious and creative, had carved many niches of success for themselves.

Certainly in Susa, as in every Persian quarter, there were ghettos—impoverished, hovel-lined pockets where less fortunate Hebrews dwelt. Perhaps Abihail, the elder, had envisioned such a neighborhood when Mordecai had encouraged him to come for a visit. But he was seeing now, as he surveyed these well-kept housefronts, that his nephew was not among the poor.

"I tried to tell you that Mordecai has climbed high in Susa," the young woman of the group objected. With a worried sigh she reached for the old man's bundle, which wriggled now in his arms. "Please, Uncle, let me carry the baby," she pleaded. "You could stumble . . . you could . . ."

"It is all right, Leah," said her husband, Moshe, who steadied the elder's uneasy gait. "Do not press him."

Abihail had been a farmer all his life, in one of Susa's small village suburbs. So had his son, as well as his brother, both of whom had died of plague many years before. Left with no family of their own, Abihail and his wife had taken in the brother's orphaned children, Mordecai and Leah, rearing them as offspring of their own love.

Never had they dreamed that the five nephews and nieces born to Leah, and whom they loved as grandchildren, would not be their last "gifts from the Lord." Like Sarah of old, who had given Abraham his Isaac, Abihail's wife became pregnant in advanced age. The swaddled infant in the wrapper was the result.

Just seven days ago the old man's wife had died while giving birth to the child. Had Abihail not seen hope for tomorrow in the newborn's perfect form and face, his heart would have died as well.

"A daughter of Israel," he whispered as he cradled the tiny girl to his bosom. "Is she not a myrtle blossom?" he crooned as he peeked between the folds of the homespun blanket, his long patriarchal beard tickling her chin.

"Hadassah," he had named her: "Myrtle," for her creamy skin, white like the bush's fragrant flowers, and her shock of deep-brown hair, dark as evergreen boughs.

Mordecai wondered at the elder's fond behavior. He had always marveled at the old man's love of tradition and heritage. Now that he saw it had a forward thrust, as well as a backward, he marveled all the more.

As for himself, if Mordecai esteemed Israel it was for personal advantage. He had learned in youth that the line of Kish, from whom he was descended, had been Hebrew nobility. Nebuchadnezzar had imported the cream of Israelite society, bringing the highest leaders and families into exile with the Jewish king, Jeconiah. The line of Kish could be traced back to King Saul himself, and many men of the clan had been notable administrators, scribes, clerks, and accountants in Israel and Judah.

Educated in the village synagogue school, Mordecai had been praised at a young age for his finesse with figures and mathematics. He would be a financial wizard, he had decided in his youthful dreams. He would sit one day in the palace gate at Susa or Persepolis, where all the greatest consultants sat. And he would make himself famous for brilliant manipulation of the market.

But Mordecai was not without a sentimental side. Though he had been promoted beyond the village walls and had now come to reside in the city, first as a merchant's bookkeeper and now as his executive stockkeeper, he had not forgotten his kin. He loved them all devoutly, and when he thought of Judaism, he considered it best expressed by close attachment to his people.

Abihail wished he saw it more spiritually than that. He had rankled when his brother named the lad Mordecai, after Marduk, god of storm. The brother had insisted that it meant nothing to do so—that he simply liked the name, and that it was a common one in the land.

"But there is much *meaning* in a name," Abihail had insisted. "The Scriptures bear this out. The lad will have much to overcome with a name like that."

To this day it rolled awkwardly off Abihail's tongue. Though proud of his nephew, he still wished the young man had an Israelite name.

The infant was beginning to whimper. Mordecai saw his sister reach anxiously for her, accustomed to mothering as she was. It had been for this very reason that he had insisted Abihail and Hadassah stay with him for a time. Leah had too many mouths to feed and too many little ones to tend. An aging and bereaved uncle along with a tiny newborn would be an unwieldy burden.

"There are women servants at home, and we are almost there now," he reminded her. "I even hired a nurse to suckle the child. Never you mind."

Leah sighed again and shook her head. She could not imagine a confirmed bachelor like her brother long enduring the trouble a baby would bring. She had tried to warn him of the nighttime crying, the colic, the diaper changes. But he had insisted.

"Abihail needs a shift of scene," Mordecai had determined. "If he grows homesick, he will return to you. But give him a few weeks."

Fireworks imported from the Indus Valley lit the New Year's sky. It was close to midnight as the little family turned the last corner for home. The palace gate was not far from here, and folk in royal chariots were descending the winding road which led from the king's house toward town. Since the king himself, his sons, and his closest companions celebrated in Persepolis, and since women of the court would not leave the acropolis at night, the ones hastening for the market square were underlings, administrative assistants, household eunuchs, and valets. They would not miss the climax of merrymaking which would follow the light display at midnight.

Most of them were already half-drunk. The little group of Jews stepped into the shadows as they went by, watching them quietly. Mordecai's lips curled in a covert smile at their frivolity. He had known a share of high times himself since abiding in Susa, but he was careful not to let Abihail know about it.

When the courtiers were nearly past, and only a band of rowdy stragglers followed, Mordecai led his people back into the street.

Perhaps it was the Jews' simple garb, shawled heads, or downcast eyes, but something in their demeanor enraged the besotted gang who stumbled into the trail of the regal parade. Mordecai would not have recognized them had they not called to him. When they hissed his name, following it with a racial epithet, he instantly knew their voices.

Assistants to the king's grand vizier, they were. Assistants to Haman, highest counselor in the land. Mordecai knew them because his own master had enrolled him in accounting courses at the vizier's royal academy.

They had never lived up to their respectable positions. Mordecai often wondered why Haman had selected them for himself. But, of course, they were very bright—and it did not hurt them that they came from monied families.

He would have ignored the racial slur, but they would not allow it. Stopping directly before his group, they impeded passage down the walkway and began to hurl more insults at him.

"Jew boy," they taunted. "Sheep trap, sand flea!" Then, spying the elderly one behind him, as well as his attractive sister, they made crude gestures with their hands.

"What's in the bundle, old man?" one laughed. "A little lamb for New Year's dinner?"

"Of course, Drusal!" another shouted. "It wouldn't be a pig. Jews don't eat 'unclean' beasts!"

The rowdies elbowed one another, doubling over with guffaws, and Abihail shielded the baby anxiously.

"Ah!" a third cried, seeing his protective action. "It must be a treasure! Let's see, Grandpa!"

When the young men grasped at the bundle, Leah shrieked and her husband pulled her to him.

"Leave us be!" Mordecai growled. "This is nothing to you."

But suddenly, spurred to violence by hours of drink, the men shot forward, pushing Leah's husband aside and pressing Abihail to the wall.

Held tightly to her old father's chest, the baby began to cry, disclosing the secret of herself. With wicked leers the men reached for the bundle, laughing "Jew baby!" and seeming ready to toss her from hand to hand.

Abihail slumped to his knees, still clutching the infant, as Mordecai and Moshe did their best to ward off Haman's boys.

Though they had no love for Jews, in a more sober mood they never would have harmed these people. The leader would never have thrown the piercing kick to the old man's head which sent Abihail sprawling to the pavement.

Leah shrieked again and grabbed the baby, who now lay squalling on the curb. The two Jewish brothers rushed at the attackers with clenched fists.

Suddenly another chariot could be heard coming down the acropolis hill. It would prove to be only the vehicle of a tardy courtier, racing to catch up with those who had passed by earlier.

But Haman's assistants, fearing the authorities, scrambled down the avenue. Though they were drunk, they were not so addlepated as to be caught in a street brawl.

Mordecai and Moshe bent down to help the uncle to his feet. Blood trickled from the old man's forehead, and an ugly bruise throbbed at his temple.

"Help is on its way," Mordecai assured him. "A chariot approaches."

But the Persian vehicle did not slow as it drew near. If the driver even noticed the stranded Jews, he did not stop to help.

There were fireworks to see, and wine to drink in the center of town. The tall white horses shot past, pulling their regal passengers to the sting of an eager whip.

Nothing could be more important than a party.

3

A princely wedding was like practice for a coronation. It would be nine more years before young Xerxes took the throne, but his prayer to marry Vashti before another 12 months elapsed had been granted. It was an auspicious occasion, calling for all the grandeur and pomp the empire could muster, and it evoked images of the day he would be crowned.

Processionals featured the elitist corps of Darius' army, machines and weapons of war, flower-strewn carriages, bevies of dancers and high-stepping horses, orchestras and bands, and wagons of gifts for the bride and groom.

The festivities would last for weeks. Though only the most privileged friends of the palace would actually witness the nuptial rites, Darius had proclaimed a reduction in taxes, release of all but the most criminal of prisoners, and a six-month rest for his troops in training.

But Mordecai was not prone to celebrate. In the darkened chamber which had once been his own bedroom, his uncle lay in a fitful sleep, unable to walk steadily or even sit for long since the blow to his head.

The accountant had seen to it that the best physicians outside the palace of Susa were made available to Abihail. But the man was old, and had only recently sustained a great loss. Though he had much to live for in his new daughter, without his wife life was bitter. The jolt of a head wound made recovery unlikely.

Leah and Moshe had returned reluctantly to their village, leaving Mordecai in charge of both the ailing uncle and the infant. But considering their limited resources, they knew Mordecai was better able to carry the burden.

Blasts of trumpets from a marching band roused Abihail. As always, his first waking thought was of Hadassah.

"She is well," the nephew assured him. "She is with the nurse."

"She should be with her mother," the elder groaned. "God above, why has my little one been put in such a strait?"

Mordecai rarely addressed the Almighty personally. Religion was best left to the rabbis and the synagogues, he reasoned. His uncle's bold conviction that Jehovah really heard, and furthermore cared, had always intrigued him. But it was good that Abihail had his faith, since he had little else in this world.

The nephew stepped near the elder's bed. Noting his perplexed glance toward the window, he was quick to explain the sounds rising from the street.

"Prince Xerxes is getting married today," he said with a smile. "All of Susa celebrates."

Abihail was not impressed with the events of Persian royalty. "A marriage of convenience, I suppose," he muttered. "Some nobleman social-climbing on the head of his daughter."

"Not this time, I hear," Mordecai laughed. "It seems that Xerxes truly loves his bride. They have been betrothed since childhood."

Abihail leaned his head back with a sigh. "Well, and what of you, son?" he asked. "Have you ever loved a woman?"

"Not to my knowledge," the bachelor grinned. "I have had no time for such things."

"You should marry," Abihail insisted. "It would do you good. And Hadassah . . . she needs a mother."

Mordecai knew he alluded to the possibility of her being orphaned. He had tried not to admit the eventuality. He had tried not to think of his own responsibility toward the child should she be left alone.

Changing the subject, Mordecai referred to the men who had put the child's future in jeopardy.

"I have reported to the palace police what happened on New Year's Eve, Uncle. I am assured that they will look into the matter, although since the culprits were Haman's boys we may never see justice."

The old man was not surprised. "It is futile to hope we could. Tell me, who is this Haman?"

"The highest of the king's advisers. And yet he is not even a Persian, I hear. He is an Agagite, a crafty one, who has won his way to the top through many lucrative decisions."

Abihail sat up suddenly, pricked by something in the revelation.

"An Agagite?" he scowled. "He calls himself this?"

"Yes," Mordecai shrugged. "He seems proud enough of the fact."

Wondering why Abihail should take the information so seriously, he listened as the old Jew recounted a bit of Israelite lore.

"King Saul, your ancestor, once had a run-in with an Amalekite named Agag. Do you recall the incident?"

Mordecai shook his head, hoping that the history lesson would be brief.

"The father of the Agagites, Haman's ancestor, he would be."

Again the younger Jew nodded. The story would be a long one, he feared, and how it could possibly bear on their own time he could not imagine.

"The Lord Jehovah had told Saul to utterly destroy the Amalekites—men, women, children, cattle, and all. But Saul took mercy on Agag, their king, and even took the spoil from the vanquished enemy—something which God said he must not do."

Mordecai stifled a yawn. The day was very hot, and he wished he might be with the other Susaites, observing the parade outside the window.

As the musicians of Darius' court marched past, row upon row of them, Abihail's voice droned on, mixing with the rhythmic drums and lulling Mordecai half asleep.

"No end of trouble have the Amalekites been all these years!" he insisted. "The blood-feud has never ceased, except for those who do not remember."

The young accountant supposed he referred to his like, for he had never known this tale. Most Jews of his generation cared little for such matters. Only Abihail and his kind, the rabid orthodox, clung to such particulars as though they still mattered.

"I doubt that Haman knows the story either," he objected, rising from his lethargy. "So what difference does it make? If the animosity is gone from both camps, there is no war."

"Ah," Abihail argued, "but there you are wrong! This shows your shortsightedness. For Jehovah sees things in a timeless frame. He has never forgotten His promises to Abraham, though many of Abraham's children have done so. Nor has He forgotten that he swore enmity against Amalek, and that Israel is obliged to stamp him out."

Mordecai frowned incredulously. "Can you possibly believe that the command given to an ancient Israelite king devolves to his descendants?" he marveled. "Saul is dead, and Agag is dead. So it is ended!"

But Abihail was not dissuaded. Rising up from his bed, he declared, as though it were self-evident, "Saul failed! Therefore the order has been unfulfilled."

Mordecai paced the room now. Such reasoning was preposterous—the product of senility. But he would not argue impersonal theology with a sick old man.

"I think I hear the baby crying," he lied. "Rest, Uncle. The parade will be over soon, and you will be able to sleep."

With a knit brow, Abihail watched Mordecai's exit. Even in the hall beyond the darkened room, the young accountant could feel the elder's sad gaze against his back.

4

Slaves with large feathered fans stood in each corner of Darius' sumptuous council chamber, trying to keep the heat at bay. No breeze had passed between the columns of the porch all afternoon, nor had any movement of air parted the long linen curtains framing the sunlit veranda.

This was the king's private consultation room, one of several palace sanctums devoted to discussions of state. Today he and two of his generals, along with his vizier, met without his other ministers being present.

His son, Xerxes, was with them, however, just as he often was when they spoke of Persia's future. The prince sat erect in a straight-backed chair, hanging on every syllable of the conversation. For today Darius spoke of Greece.

While their great ancestor, Cyrus, had made an unprecedented move to wrest the Middle East from the Medes and Babylonians, consolidating the empire under one banner and founding what would become the greatest dominion on earth, Darius' genius lay in the fact that he completed the organization of the realm created by his predecessors.

From the extremities of the East to the rim of the Mediterranean he had expanded the empire, constructing a canal from the Nile to the Red Sea and even sending an expedition down the Indus to explore the Indian Ocean. For the first time ever there was a commercial waterway linking India, Persia, and Egypt, so that Darius' sovereignty was more vast than any which had gone before.

It was therefore fitting that he was known as "Darius, one king of many, one lord of many, the great king, king of kings, king of the countries possessing all kinds of people, king of this great earth far and wide."

But he was not content. He never would be until the Aegean and the Hellenistic world lay at his feet.

Some said a demon drove Darius. His forerunners had been great warlords. Cyrus had died fighting a savage Eastern race, and Cambyses had made bold attempts against Ethiopia. But Darius had been the first to invade the West.

Trekking into the Danube territory 22 years ago he had made the first historic attack of Asia on Europe. Sweeping through the Balkan hinterland, he crossed the great river on a bridge of boats, and though revolt among his own men ended the campaign in failure, the Greeks and Scythians could no longer consider the Persian dynasty a slumbering dog.

The men in the room today were privileged with a view of the harem courtyard, spread directly before them at the veranda's foot. Few men on earth were allowed to view the king's women. It was supposedly against the law for anyone to look upon his queen. But, though dozens of concubines and secondary wives sported in the pools and garden, the men rarely glanced their way.

Intensely involved in conversation, the generals leaned forward, riveted by the king's ambition. Otanes, Vashti's father, and Mardonius, the mightiest of Persia's military advisers, had much to gain by being here. And Haman, whose expertise lay not in war and weapons but in finance, could advance himself even further in the emperor's graces by wise contributions regarding the state of Persia's economy.

Years before, Otanes had proven his indispensable worth as a warlord when he had subdued Byzantium and her sister cities, securing the entire border between the Asian and European continents and bringing Persia's frontiers within easy distance of Greece.

In the meantime, several forays at Sardes, Miletus, Cyprus, and Caria had thrown victory from hand to hand between the Persians and Greeks. When a surprise nighttime maneuver had destroyed the entire Persian force at Caria, generals and all, the Westerners won a two-year respite by land and sea. Defeat of the Persian fleet at Cyprus and the army at Caria had forced the Persians into a palsied stance, and months had passed with no retaliation on Darius' part.

Perhaps today's meeting heralded a revival of courage on the king's part. Mardonius was hot for blood, and Otanes itched for the feel of the spear.

"How do you see the Greeks these days?" Darius asked his generals. "What are the reports from the Aegean?"

Mardonius cleared his throat and rubbed his hands upon his tight trousers. "The Greeks lack leadership. They are disunited," he replied.

Otanes nodded, adding eagerly, "They have not used their time well during these two years. There are no signs of movement against the sea. They seem to have been simply resting all these months."

The king smiled and leaned back into his throne. The consultants almost laughed with him, but they would not presume to do so just yet.

"They are at rest? But they won the last skirmish. Why would *they* need to recuperate?"

"Our successes have consistently outnumbered theirs, Your Majesty," Mardonius reminded him. "Their victories have been short-lived, or by surprise advantage. They know we could crush them if we had half a mind . . ."

Otanes fidgeted uneasily at this and Mardonius caught himself before he said too much. His suggestion bordered on the discourteous. No one dared impute cowardice to Darius.

Of course, all present knew the question should not have been why the Greeks had been "resting," but why Persia had made no offensive in the same length of time. This was Darius' matter alone, but all suspected that he had taken his fill of beatings at the hands of the Greeks, and was only now recovering.

The emperor scowled at Mardonius, and the general cast his gaze to the floor. When the king addressed Haman next, the warlord's flushed face began to cool.

"The treasury is adequate to an expedition?" Darius inquired.

Such a question! Did the emperor really wonder if the wealthiest coffers on earth could sustain a venture against the West? The generals glanced at one another covertly as Haman joined the talk.

Of course they knew the vizier had been invited only to give the final seal to the king's desires. Everyone knew there was no financial trouble in Persia. But Haman must make good his reason for being here.

"Your Highness has recently reduced taxes," he began. "They may need to be levied at the higher rate once more."

Xerxes shot a keen look in Haman's direction. The citizens of Persia had been granted a break in tribute and celebration of the prince's recent wedding. Was the vizier suggesting that the court had made a mistake?

Otanes, whose daughter was the object of the celebration, liked the insinuation no more than Xerxes. But he dared say nothing, as Haman was the king's favorite.

Darius did not always agree with Haman, however. Studying the young bridegroom fondly, he shook his head. "Taxes shall remain untouched for the time established," he asserted. And Otanes nodded to Xerxes, very pleased.

Haman kept his silence as Mardonius dealt with matters more important to the moment.

"We can engage a Phoenician fleet," he asserted, "and we can call upon contingents from Egypt, Cilicia, and Cyprus to invade Greek waters. All we need is time."

Xerxes' blood boiled with ambition as the commanders plotted their course. Perhaps one day, when he entered upon the throne, he would rule the Western world as well as the Eastern.

Surveying the harem through the consultants' bent heads, he imagined Vashti crowned with the jewels of Greece and Rome, Athens and Carthage.

He would give her half his kingdom. Whichever half she desired.

5

Mordecai, the Jew, stood upon his little veranda watching as the troops of Darius returned from war. He could see just enough through the narrow grates of his barred gate to tell him it was a sorry scene in the street tonight.

Hadassah, his adopted daughter, played at the feet of her governess, pulling at the tall stalks of lilies bordering Mordecai's modest garden. The music of the small fountain which babbled in his court was drowned out by the slow tramping of soldiers and the rhythm of funeral-like drums proceeding down the avenue. But the little girl, now three years old, was oblivious to the great dishonor received by Persia's troops at the hands of the Greeks.

Her father, were he still alive, would have told her that Darius had been retributed by the hand of God, that it was Jehovah who had seen to Persia's defeat due to its greed and materialism.

He would have told her that the 6400 Persian dead at Marathon, versus only 192 lost on the Greek side, was reminiscent of the battles of the Hebrews at Jericho and Abraham at Dan. He would have told her that such things do not happen without supernatural intervention. After numerous victories in the Aegean region, and the taking of whole cities of Greek slaves, the Persians had seemed invincible. God had a way of laughing last, Abihail would have told her. The old man had died shortly after coming to Susa, however. So now there was no one to teach Hadassah the deepest things of Judaism.

But the fact that Mordecai was weak on religious training was no indication of his feelings toward the child. The tiny girl had filled a spot in the stubborn bachelor's heart which he had not known was vacant. With the passing months, as he had seen her take her first steps and learn her first words, his affections had expanded.

Along with this came a distinct antipathy toward Haman, the man whose underlings had orphaned the child. When, as Abihail had predicted, nothing was done by the palace police to bring justice against the young men, Mordecai had found himself increasingly doubtful of Persian policy toward the Jews, and especially skeptical of the grand vizier. Though generations ago King Cyrus had emancipated the Hebrew people, it seemed that justice was still elusive.

Nonetheless, Mordecai rarely considered Abihail's adamant assertions concerning the "sons of Agag." The old man's view of history and nations was too ludicrous to be taken seriously.

The only heritage of value given him by his uncle was the curly-haired child who clutched now at his robe. In her tiny dimpled fist she held forth a long-stemmed lily, offering it to Mordecai.

"A scepter befitting a queen," he said with a grin, as he reached down for her and lofted her to his shoulder. Pointing to the bedraggled spearmen who marched past the gate, he teased, "Poor, poor warriors. Perhaps if you had touched them with your wand, Hadassah, they would have come home victors."

* * *

King Darius longed to revenge the rebuff at Marathon. He longed to annex Greece. His most restless neighbors would have made his most useful subjects. But the king whose empire had spread as far as possible to the east, north, and south would not live to recoup his Western losses.

Five years after the defeat in the Aegean, Darius was dead. Whether he was a good or an evil man would remain forever open to debate. As for Xerxes, he would do well to emulate his father in many things. And from the start, as he watched the funeral procession of the fallen monarch, he determined to do so.

The 27-year-old prince rode this evening in a golden carriage behind the black-shrouded wagon which bore his father's corpse into the Zagros Mountains. Far behind lay the glow of Susa, coral in the setting winter sun. Beside him sat his wife, her hand resting lightly upon his knee.

Before Darius' body would be interred in the ancestral tombs at Persepolis, his spirit would be committed to Ahura-Mazda, god of the sky.

It had to be said of Darius that, though he was devoted to this one deity, he gave amazing latitude to the other religions of his diverse subjects. Imitating Cyrus, he even saw to it that the temples and worship of all gods were subsidized by the state.

But when it came to his private devotions, the god embraced by Zoroaster, famed and obscure prophet of the Zagros, was his sole focus. His religion did not call for much art or architecture. No soaring temples lifted the minds of the faithful to the deity. Sufficient were small fire altars atop lofty peaks in the untamed wilderness of Persia's barbaric ancestors.

Through the dusk Xerxes and Vashti could see the curl of gray smoke ascending from one such pyre lit at the crest of the jagged, snow-covered horizon. The flash of burning coals was visible, and behind the pale light, which intruded even at this distance into the darkness, they could make out the silhouettes of the magi, men of the priestly caste, who would offer up Darius' soul.

Certain elements of Persia's religion lingered from the time before Zoroaster's teachings, from the time of the Aryans, ancient animists who had once inhabited the hinterland. Though Zoroaster had recognized no nature worship, some customs died hard.

In keeping with those old traditions, therefore, Darius' body would be exposed to the mountain frost until sunrise, while the magi spread the flesh of a small sacrifice upon a carpet of herbs and burned it to the chant of a theogony.

Already the haunting drone of the hymn was borne on the cool wind descending from the peak. Xerxes felt a chill cross his shoulders, but would not admit to his wife that he found the priests and their rituals an eerie combination.

The shadow of a hawk crossed the icy moon directly above the prince's path as the carriage driver urged the horses higher. A good omen or bad? he wondered. The priests, who studied such matters, would have known, for they saw omens in everything.

Xerxes lifted his regal face to the mountain. Pale silver light illumined his noble features and played against his crimped beard like the hoarfrost of venerable age. He was, in fact, feeling far older than 27 tonight. The knowledge that tomorrow he would receive the imperial crown was a weighty burden. Perhaps with daylight he would feel the joy of power and prestige unequaled in the world. But tonight, grief and responsibility pressed him down.

Cradling Vashti's small hand in his own, he glanced down at her supple fingers, the warmth of her touch strangely saddening him. Dependent she was, as a bird. His most prized possession, though he possessed all things.

As the refrain of the priestly chorus reached them, tears rose to his eyes.

"Ahura-Mazda, who upholds the earth and the firmament," it rang, "who causes the moon to wax and wane, who yokes swiftness to wind and cloud, who creates light and dark, sleeping and waking, morning, noon, and night . . ."

If there were a god in heaven, a father-god, he would surely fit this description, Xerxes believed. But tonight he knew only emptiness. On the eve of his coronation he felt inadequate to his calling.

At last the little processional reached the zenith of the hill. With careful hands the priests pulled back the dark shroud which concealed Darius' prone form, and then, in memory of the days when a corpse would have been left for the dogs and vultures, they ceremonially tore his neckline.

Xerxes stared into the air above his father's frigid body, almost hoping to see the spirit thus released. Such thoughts he kept to himself, shamed by their childishness.

But when the chant began again, and when the flames of the sacrifice leapt renewed into the coolness, his throat was tight.

"Ahura-Mazda," the chorus swelled, "who created this earth, who created yonder heaven, who created man, who created welfare for man . . ."

Scarcely could he bear to hear more. Though it was not dignified to do so, he clung to Vashti's hand and lifted it to his lips. The nearness of her at this needy moment, the availability of her love, filled him with hope.

Perhaps he could be what he must be.

The priests and the entourage of courtiers were fixed on the spectacle of ritual and invocation. They would not see if the prince were to hold her close.

Pressing her head to his breast, he touched his lips to her soft dark hair.

"Precious," he whispered. "My most precious possession."

ESTHER

PART II
Pride Before a Fall

6

"A tax farmer!" Mordecai bellowed. "I have heard it with my own ears. Haman is a tax farmer!"

Leah stood over the pan of dirty cups and utensils, cleaning up after yet another meal. Her children, all teenagers or nearly so, had accomplished their afternoon chores and had taken off for various parts of the village. She, looking forward to an evening of adult conversation, listened eagerly to Mordecai's palace gossip.

Her brother, within the first two years of the new administration, had risen from merchant's stockkeeper to executive of inventory in the royal house. She had always been proud of Mordecai, but never more than now.

"So how did you learn this?" she marveled. "Do you have access to Haman's books?"

"Not directly," he explained. "But there are few secrets among the management. Haman weasled his way into Darius' graces years ago by buying up provincial concessions."

"He is a tax collector, then," she sneered.

"More than that. A tax *farmer* actually pays an annual lump sum for the right to bleed the public. He does not just earn a commission. He pays such a high rate for the privilege that he is allowed to keep the entire collection! Can you imagine the returns? Enormous!"

Mordecai slapped his thighs and threw his head back. "Tens of thousands of talents!" he sighed.

Leah shook her head. "Then our tax monies, given by the sweat of our brows, do not even go to the royal treasuries?"

"Oh, be assured, the king makes a haul off the bidders. He does not sell the concessions for a song. With several sharing the rights to each province, he makes as much as or more than the taxes would bring in. And the competition between the concessionaires . . ." Here he pounded a fist into his open palm. "They would kill to beat one another out."

Leah pulled the wet dishes from the suds and rinsed them in another bucket. "Folk have been known to murder for less."

Mordecai knew she referred to the wanton violence directed against Abihail. Rising from the low stool in her kitchen, he walked to the little window which looked across the fields east of the village. The snow-capped Zagros Mountains loomed majestic and protective above the sweeping valley.

Mordecai loved Persia, but often, as Hadassah had grown, he had found his mind turning to the teachings of his uncle, especially to his tales of Israel, passed down from his own father and his before him.

He wondered if Israel were as beautiful as the land of his birth. And he wondered if he had missed out on something wonderful by passing off his heritage so lightly.

In the flowered field beyond the low town gate, village children played. Hadassah, now ten years old, ran with the smallest as they mimicked the adult game of goat-drag, riding sticks like horses and hauling a stuffed burlap bag from stake to stake on a miniature playing field. Never was the girl happier than when she visited her second cousins, the energetic offspring of Mordecai's sister.

As the accountant watched her run through the ankle-high grass, her slender legs kicking up dust and her long raven curls bouncing, he knew he would do best by the child to afford her more exposure to the Jewish community.

"She is nearly a young lady . . ." he mused.

Leah, surprised by the new topic, glanced with him out the window. "You are only now noticing?" she teased. "Look over there," she pointed, indicating her 15-year-old firstborn son, who leaned against the gate cavalierly. "David has certainly noticed already."

Mordecai nodded, a smile working at this lips. "I would like to bring her here more often," he requested.

"Of course!" Leah offered. "You know we all enjoy her!"

"Then it is settled," the brother determined. "It would be good for all of us to keep closer ties. I would like her to visit at least twice a month. She would be no trouble. I will pay you . . ."

"Nonsense!" Leah protested. "*Pay*, for *family*? I won't hear of it. And, of course she is obedient! Docile as a doe!"

Turning for her dishpan again, she bustled to finish her work before sunset, shaking her head and muttering exasperation about brothers and about men in general.

* * *

Indeed David, the eldest of Leah's children, *had* noticed Hadassah. She had always been a comely child, and now, as she approached young womanhood, her charms were of another sort.

Sitting cross-legged on the ground, his back against the gate-post, he watched her keenly as she sported with the younger children of the neighborhood. Mordecai had never allowed her to wear her hair twisted and fettered, as so many of the haughty girls of Susa wore theirs. For this David was never more grateful than at this moment as it swung free in the breeze, glancing against her rosy cheeks and caressing her back with brown-black waves. Where the descending sun caught it, auburn-to-red tones revealed themselves amid the curls tumbling about her shoulders.

Nor had Mordecai ever allowed Hadassah's hair to be cut. Though it was trimmed fashionably about the face, it flowed to her midback and bore no ribbons or pins.

Pale lavender gowns were unusual in the small hamlet where David had been raised. The fact that Hadassah's simple dress was out of this hue, and was girded with a fine linen rope, marked her as one of Susa's upper middle class. Whenever she came to visit the village, younger children stood in awe of her as much for this fact as for her unusual beauty.

Always their star-struck gazes mellowed to open smiles, however, when the gentle girl took them by the hands and began to play with them.

Just now, as the stuffed burlap bag (the pretend goat) was carried by an opponent toward the enemy's goal, she raced after the rider, not as quickly as she might, but fast enough to give him a challenge. From behind came another opponent on chubby legs, grasping for her to take her to the ground.

He succeeded only in snapping the belt about her slender waist, breaking the clasp on her fine-carved alabaster buckle.

Squealing, Hadassah wheeled about and confronted the challenger, feigning more offense than she felt.

As she bent over to pick up the broken treasure, David leapt to his feet and ran to her. "Let me see," he offered, touching her lightly on the arm. When she rose to find her cousin brooding over her, a blush rose to her cheeks.

Handing the buckle to him, she said nothing. As he turned the ornament over and over in his hands, she was struck by the glints of gold within his azure eyes.

"This is a very fine piece," he marveled.

"Papa gave it to me," she said, finding her voice.

David nodded. "It must be a pleasure to give you fine things," he said.

Hadassah was not too young to detect the admiration in his tone. But not being trained in worldly ways, she did not know how to respond.

"It is a Greek design, is it not?" David observed, still contemplating the jewel.

"I believe so," Hadassah replied, surprised at his apparent knowledge of such things, and not really certain herself of the artistic origins.

"We have Greek blood in our veins as well as Jewish," he went on. "Did you know this?"

Hadassah recalled Mordecai's allusions to the family's mixed roots. "Such a thing is not unusual," she replied.

"No," David agreed.

But when Hadassah saw that he was proud of the fact, she quickly added, "Of course, you have acquired the look as well as the blood."

The young man straightened his shoulders and lifted his strong chin. He had hoped she noticed, and that she approved. Blond hair and blue eyes were rare in Persia, and had won him the admiration of many village girls.

"I think I can fix this for you," he asserted. "I am an artist in my own right, though I shall likely always be a farmer."

Hadassah was touched by his youthful frustration. "Papa left the village to work in Susa," she reminded him. "Aunt Leah says you are gifted with carving and painting. Perhaps . . ."

"No," David said again. "I am needed too much here."

The girl looked at the brothers and sisters who had congregated at David's back. They had come out from the house to call the two cousins home.

Darkness was descending quickly now, as it always did in the desert. As the family walked toward Leah's warmly lit house, Hadassah knew that David spoke the truth. His parents would require his assistance for a long time. He might never be able to pursue a career beyond the village gate.

Though she was very young, Hadassah felt a peculiar stirring in her as she followed David's manly lead back to the cottage. It was not the first time she had felt it. She had not failed to notice his ruddy strength and field-hardened physique. His golden hair and eyes only added to his appeal.

He still held the buckle in his artistic fingers. She watched him study it as they walked. No words passed between them, but Hadassah stayed close to his elbow.

7

In following Darius' love of Ahura-Mazda and his prophet, Zoroaster, Xerxes had departed from his father's ways in one unusual respect: He had chosen to have no harem, but to honor a monogamous relationship with his beloved wife, Vashti.

Zoroaster had taught that the highest good was symbolized between humans in faithful love for one's spouse. Where Persian kings turned from this injunction, they deviated from the noblest path.

As soon as Xerxes had taken the throne, he set about to send the women away, seeing to it that they were endowed with gifts of precious metal, fabrics, and spices so that they might have means of support. He could do nothing about the fact that many of them, no matter how lovely they might be, would never find a husband. Virginity was highly prized in a bride, something none of them could claim. And to have lived under the same roof as the king, though supposedly an honor, had marked them as "soiled" women.

Harem girls, once turned away, would not even qualify as widows, but would be considered "scorned" women, rendering them even less valuable.

Still, Xerxes could not help this. It was better to remove them, he reasoned, than to maintain secondary wives against the teachings of his faith.

Hadassah had been allowed this morning to enter the outer rim of buildings in the palace area. Mordecai was in charge of an inventory tour through the storehouses of the acropolis, and he had brought his adopted daughter with him for the day, leaving her to enjoy the sights as he escorted his young accountants about their assignments.

Never had the girl been privileged to see the inner workings of the royal compounds. Of course, nothing private to the king's family transpired in the utilitarian courts enclosing the monarch's private palace. Nonetheless, it was an honor for her to be here.

Mordecai was presently inspecting the second floor of the royal warehouse where the king kept his most prized gold pieces. Resting in cases of velvet were tiny trinkets shaped like striding lions, miniature bulls, and birds of prey. Each was worth more than its weight in artistic beauty alone. Thousands upon thousands of delicate chains, bracelets, rings, and earrings sat unused in cedar boxes, the containers themselves worth a fortune.

Once a year the inventory must be recounted, valued, and polished. This was not the rule of a miser, but rather the wisdom of a long line of Persian kings who, despite their wealth, kept careful books. For the managers of the coffers, the day the accountants came around was a tense time. If any treasure was missing, even the slightest piece, it could mean their lives.

Of course, Hadassah was not privy to her uncle's work. She had been permitted to ascend to the second story, but had been left outside the labyrinth of doors barring strangers from the treasury rooms.

The glory of even the limited area she observed, however, was enough to occupy her for hours. The shiny marble balcony, wide enough for two chariots, and the intricate carvings of the turquoise-inlaid mezzanine filled her with wonder. A small garden below, leading to the outer gate of the compound, dazzled her with poppies, irises, flamingos, and fountains. Were she never to see another inch of the acropolis, her memory would be entertained for a lifetime.

When the sound of soft voices caught her attention, she stood poised at the rail, marveling at beauty even more splendid than the surroundings. Half-a-dozen women had entered the little gateway garden. In flowing silken gowns they passed beneath Hadassah's gaze, slender as flower stalks. The girl had seen lovely ladies in Susa's streets, but none so glamorous as these. Soft hair of various hues framed faces that no artist could have conceived. Yet great art was evident in arched eyebrows, blushed cheeks, and red lips. Paint accentuated eyes already large by nature, shading and highlighting flawless complexions.

While each lady had individual charm, they were more alike than not. Hadassah was not too young to realize that these must be women of the king's harem, all selected to suit the taste of one man.

Long of limb and graceful as willows, most of them were quite tall. In carriage and in form they could have passed for sisters, though their skin tones told that they were of different nationalities. The young girl did not know much about the world, but she had heard of Babylon and Africa and India, and figured that these women represented such farflung places.

Captivated, she observed them with the same fascination that the village children exhibited whenever she herself graced their humble town.

But, while she would have expected great happiness to accompany such beauty, these ladies appeared anything but cheerful.

Tears smudged charcoaled eyes and heavy sorrow contorted winsome lips. A few of the women had locked arms, as though for support, and muffled weeping rose from the group.

As the klatch of women crossed the garden, drawing near the door to the outer world, several began to wail miserably. On the instant, a stern-looking character entered behind them.

"Such clatter will not be tolerated!" he growled, his bald head flushed crimson from ear to ear. It seemed he would strike at them, and Hadassah knew he could send them all sprawling with a blow, for he was a big, meaty man, his bare biceps sporting bracelets which would fit a harem girl's waist.

Falling against each other, the ladies cried out and then stifled themselves.

Suddenly the sound of quick footsteps approaching from the corridor halted the bully. The women dried their eyes, falling to their knees, just as he did.

The footsteps heralded the approach of another woman, who stood now in the doorway. Hadassah, peering down between the banister posts, could not have imagined anyone more beautiful than the girls who huddled together. Yet the newcomer to whom they made obeisance was even more ravishing.

"Your Majesty . . ." the hulking fellow cried, "live forever!"

The young spectator deduced immediately that it was the Queen of Persia who stood beneath her gaze. And her small-girl heart tripped with awe.

All her life she had heard of Vashti. She had heard of her great beauty, but she had never dreamed she would one day see it for herself.

It was not Vashti's clothing, nor the style of her hair, nor the flair of her cosmetics which set her apart. Rather, it was her bearing, her noble demeanor, her look of certainty, which elevated her.

Ignoring the fawning man at her feet, she hastened to the cowering women, whose tears for now were fearfully contained.

"Stand, sisters," she commanded.

The ladies, confounded, did so. Then the queen glared at their keeper, who had not dared to look up from the floor.

"Angus!" she confronted him. "Have I not spoken with you about your handling of the harem? You shall treat these women with the same respect they merited when Darius was their lord."

Since the behemoth was being addressed, he knew he must rise and face the queen. How to account for himself he knew not. Vashti realized that any vulnerable female was a temptation to his cruel nature. But he had been raised to his position, keeper of the concubines, by Darius. And, while this station would terminate as soon as the women were removed, only Xerxes, and not Vashti, could send him from the palace.

Nonetheless, he must treat the queen with respect or else lose his head, if not further employment.

"Your Majesty, the women are contrary," he lied. "They require a firm hand."

At this the ladies, who had done nothing amiss, turned defensive eyes to the queen.

"I think they have done no wrong," Vashti interposed. "See that *you* do nothing but your proper job."

Then, clapping her hands, she went toward the hall door and summoned a small train of servants.

Once again the girl on the balcony had reason to marvel as a cohort of slaves entered the garden, each bearing a trayload of luxuries.

Flasks of jasmine, gold necklaces, cakes of myrrh and aloe, sachets of spices, and jeweled bracelets were piled upon broad silver dishes. Hadassah did not know much about the worth of such finery, but she was sure Mordecai would value it at a very great price.

The women, awestruck as each was handed her own trayful of treasure, reacted as though the offerings were worth a lifetime of acquisition.

Trembling, some of them refused the gifts, scarcely believing the queen could mean such generosity. But at last, as Vashti implored them, they conceded, tears dripping down their faces.

"These should stand you in good stead until you can establish yourselves," she explained.

Establish themselves? Hadassah thought. *They should never have to lift a finger the rest of their lives!*

"Though the king has foregone more than one wife," the queen went on, "he would not send you forth into poverty."

"But, Your Highness," one of the girls objected, "these are from your *own* storehouse! They are not a man's treasures."

"Hush, Darla," another softly warned. "You have not been addressed."

But the queen took no notice. Clapping again, she sent the servants away.

"Take them forth now, Angus," Vashti commanded. "See that they all find lodging, and see to it that their treasures are put in safe keeping."

By this she referred to the fact that the poor women, unlearned in matters of investment, might abuse their endowments or, even worse, lose them to thieves within hours of leaving the grounds.

"I am your servant, Majesty," Angus replied, bowing as he led the ladies through the outer door.

Hadassah sat very still upon the balcony. The beauty of the women and the glory of the gifts had riveted her so that she could not pull away.

When Vashti had sent the slaves back down the hall she stood alone for a long moment, looking toward the door where the ladies had departed. Tears glimmered along her lashes, and the girl on the balcony held her breath, deeply moved by the queen's compassion.

What drew Vashti's gaze upward, toward the mezzanine, she would never know. But suddenly the sad eyes were upon Hadassah. The girl trembled, not knowing what punishment her eavesdropping might deserve.

Soon enough it was apparent, however, that the queen would dismiss the child's indiscretion. In her expression was only bemused surprise, as though she wondered how the young girl had come to be spying.

And then the expression turned to wonder. But Hadassah could not interpret this, for she did not fully appreciate her own charms.

Vashti did. The queen knew what loveliness was, seeing it every day about the courts and possessing it herself. The queen knew that, had this child been older, and a member of the harem, the king would have found it very hard to disown her.

8

Vashti observed the banquet preparations with mixed emotions. For a full three years Xerxes had been obsessed with plans to invade Greece. Once he had taken the throne, set his administration in order, and sent the harem away, he had turned his mind to the West with a vengeance that frightened his queen.

Now he was about to launch his expansionism, and to celebrate he had sent invitations to the 127 provinces under his rule, calling for the chief leaders and noblemen from throughout his empire to attend a six-month party in Susa.

Already thousands were arriving for the festivities, which would begin in a few days. 40,000 anticipated visitors would stay for varying lengths of time, arriving and departing throughout the festival.

Of course, the event would be honored by the entire city, as hostels and homes were opened to accommodate the influx. Local merchants rallied to prepare for the boost that such an event would be for the economy. People worked day and night to produce wares for purchase by the incoming tourists. From shoe merchants to jewelers, from bakers to perfumers, all made ready.

As for the palace itself, the inner court, or pavilion, would be the scene of the king's banquet. This open, colonnaded garden could be intensely hot in summer, but Xerxes planned to station a hundred slaves about the garden's numerous fountains, where they would fan the guests with imported ostrich plumes day and night.

Vashti stood upon the upper deck of the court, gazing across the sumptuous arboretum. Servants scurried amid flowering bushes and trees, arranging furniture and spreading pristine linens upon the tables. The colors decorating the extravaganza were of cool hues: Curtains of white, green, and blue were fastened to silver rings upon the marble pillars and were bound together by cords of royal violet. Chaises in the same fabrics were placed along the tables, their gold and silver frames resting upon decks of purple, blue, white, and gleaming black marble.

Xerxes had recently squelched insurrections in Egypt and Babylon. He had inflicted harsh penalties upon those states, leveling the Babylonian temple and melting to bullion their 1800-pound statue to Marduk.

These successes had piqued his appetite for further conquest, drawing his energies toward the West.

His wife, chief treasure of his heart, received less and less of his time as he pursued his dreams. It had begun in small things—tardiness to a rendezvous, the overlooking of an anniversary. Now their stolen moments were fewer and fewer, his attention span more fleeting.

Vashti had just come from the women's court, where her own banquet was being prepared. Only women of the palace, wives and daughters of the invited noblemen, would be attending her feast, which would likewise last for days. But it would be a tame, ladylike affair, unlike the boisterous and ribald merrymaking which would dominate the king's strictly male festivities.

As the headwaiter emerged from the palace's enormous pantry, leading a bevy of slaves, Vashti grew uneasy. Each slave hauled a small wheeled cart, piled high with gold drinking horns, every one of a different configuration, from winged griffins to strutting bears. This would be a drinking orgy unlike any held here before. And she hesitated to think of the excesses it would inspire.

Her husband had been busy all day with the governor of the feast, looking into the man's plans and adding to them. Vashti had not expected to see him this afternoon, and when he entered the court, across the way, she thought he might at last have a moment for her.

But it was not to be.

"Leave room along here," he was saying as the governor followed behind him. "Move in this row of tables so that my treasures may be paraded."

"Just so, Your Majesty," the governor agreed, clapping his hands and sending servants to reposition the furniture.

"The finest riches of the warehouse shall be brought forth for display, borne aloft upon silver trays or hauled in gilded barrows," Xerxes continued, his voice trailing down the hall.

Could he mean it? Vashti marveled, wondering at his compulsive pride. Such an exhibition could take weeks!

Once, she recalled, she had been considered his most precious possession. But today he had not even seen her standing alone, waiting for him.

Sadly she turned for her chamber, fearing another night without him.

9

Lights danced in the court of King Xerxes, potted candles on bobbing trays borne high on the shoulders of slaves, who dipped to serve as they wove between tables and couches.

It was the last week of Xerxes' feast, the evening of the seventh day. At least a thousand men had been served in the garden since morning, congregating in shifts to celebrate the culmination of half a year of merrymaking.

This was the final spate of excess, capping the previous six months of orgiastic feasting and drinking which had entertained notables from about the empire. And this week was reserved for the king's own, those who served his personal and state needs, from janitors to cabinet officials, in the palace itself.

As the candles spun a hypnotic web about the guests, the music of pipes and lutes and timbrels evoked enchanting delirium.

Of course, so did the wine. By pitchers and casks and buckets it flowed—into the golden chalices shaped in many shapes, down the mouths and throats of ten hundred laughing men.

"To Xerxes!" the toast rang, followed by clanking rims of tankard on tankard. "To Persia!" "To Mardonius!" "To Otanes!" "To War!" chased by clinks and gulps and cheers.

Jokes flowed too, and dares and taunts and jibes. From time to time, females imported from about the king's immense realm danced and teased and cavorted. They were not women of the palace, the king having removed his harem, and the ladies who now graced the ground of Vashti's banquet, wives and daughters of palace officials, would have been offended at such an invitation.

The fleshy bouquet of scantily clad dancers greeted an increasingly lusty crowd each time they were summoned, their presence stirring the room to ever-higher pitches of demand and appreciation.

Between the pageantry of the women appeared precisioned jugglers, hilarious clowns, and dexterous acrobats for the audience's pleasure. All the while, as the wine flowed and the delicacies of the king's kitchen were gorged upon, the treasures of the monarch were paraded in the background—furs never worn, cutlery and weaponry never brandished, diamonds and jewels never sported, fabulous works of art, and rare birds and animals from every corner of the empire.

For half a year these valuables had been displayed through the court, and now as the party was winding down, the king, besotted, gazed upon the end of their procession with heavy-lidded eyes.

He was deliciously relaxed as he lay back upon his chaise, high upon the uppermost deck of the court. But his closest valets, who knew him best, could see that he grew restless.

His plans to go against the West, hinted at numerous times in the previous six months, had finally been heralded privately before his own palace cohorts. Now he seemed anxious for action.

As clearly as he could think in his drunken condition, he tried to imagine some very spectacular way to climax this final evening of the most elaborate celebration which the world had ever seen.

His valets, middle-aged eunuchs with smooth faces and boyish voices, congregated at his back, sensing his regal agitation.

As the monarch rose upon one elbow, resting his pensive face upon his fist, he gestured for Mehuman, his chief valet, and the gaunt fellow hastened forward, bowing to the ground.

Xerxes, scarcely looking at him, stroked his head and patted him upon the cheek. "These are all my very best friends," he slurred, tears in his royal eyes as he scanned the loud revelers below.

"Yes, Your Majesty," Mehuman agreed.

"I have done so little for them," the king remorsed, weaving a bit upon his bed.

"But, sir," Mehuman objected, "you have reserved the finest for these folk. This week has been the highlight of the year."

"No, no," Xerxes insisted, flicking a long hand in the eunuch's peach-clean face. "They deserve more—something I have done for no one else, and shall never do again."

By now the other valets, nervous over the king's unhappiness, had gathered behind Mehuman. Biztha, Harbona, Bigtha, Abagtha, Zethar, and Carkas pressed close to the chief eunuch's bowed form, and each in turn received a stroke upon his bent head from the unusually affectionate emperor.

"What can we do for His Majesty?" they inquired, seeing that he was determined to have something.

"His Majesty desires to grace these revelers with some extraordinary benevolence," Mehuman explained. "He has shown them his treasures and bestowed upon them royal gifts, the finest wines and rarest delicacies from his larder. Yet he wishes to do more."

"Such is the nature of His Majesty's generous spirit," Harbona purred.

"Most Benevolent Lord," Zethar offered, "perhaps a tour of your grounds . . ."

"They have all seen the grounds!" Mehuman quickly corrected, seeing Xerxes' furrowed brow.

"Rings for their fingers," Carkas suggested.

"He has given fine jewelry to them all!" Mehuman replied, gesturing to a thousand braceleted arms and necklaced breasts.

In a huddle, the valets continued to confer but came up with nothing. At last Mehuman, frustrated, shrugged and said, "Your Highness, we can imagine nothing which you have not already given. You have bestowed food for their lips, wine for their hearts, song for their ears, women for their eyes . . ."

At this Xerxes lurched forward, his crimped beard quivering as his head shook. "No, no!" he cried. "I have been selfish! There is yet one thing I have withheld from my friends, from those who would give their life's blood for me!"

The king exaggerated, not about his generosity but about the loyalty of his companions. However, Mehuman dared not challenge his wine-dazzled estimation.

"All the women in the world would not be enough to honor my dearest allies," Xerxes enthused. "Had I given them my harem, it would not have been sufficient!"

Xerxes rode high on the excitement of six months, on the daring of future campaigns and on the praise of his plans for expansion. He soared on wings of wine and the sound of laughter swelling up from the court.

His multitude of comrades did not attend to him just now, for they were busy with the licentious freedom of the seven-day fling. Never would they or his valets dream that he was about to break one of the most stubborn taboos of his ancestors for their sake.

"Only one woman can do justice to the king's desire. Only Vashti herself, my chief treasure, is good enough for such friends!" Xerxes declared.

Mehuman drew a sharp breath.

"You cannot mean . . ."

"Bring her forth!" Xerxes commanded.

Suddenly a pall of silence overtook the eunuchs. The guests below, ignorant of the proposition, went on with their hilarity unimpeded. But the valets were appalled.

"Your Highness," Harbona dared to remind him, "it is the law that no man apart from the emperor himself is to look upon the queen."

Yes—this was the law. It was impossible that she would be spared the gazes of all men whatsoever, exposed as she was to life in the palace, but the spirit of the injunction applied against men looking upon her to lust after her.

Still, Xerxes darted a threatening glance at the disapproving Harbona.

"Am I a child, that my eunuchs are my counselors?" the emperor snarled. "I said, 'Bring her forth!' "

"Your Majesty, how shall we summon her? What shall we say?" Mehuman hedged.

"Say, 'Your husband desires your presence in the garden!' " Xerxes replied, his tone tinged with sarcasm. "What do you suppose you should say?"

"Do you simply wish for her to appear? And nothing more?" the valet hoped.

Xerxes, reading his apprehension, grew impatient. "What evil do you imagine of me?" he said with a glare. "Tell the queen to place the royal crown upon her head, so that all the men may gaze upon her beauty! She is a very beautiful woman!"

Mehuman bowed, agreeing utterly with his assessment, but still uneasy over the results of such an appearance before this disorderly mob.

"If you feel this is wisdom . . ."

"Are you questioning my sagacity or my sobriety?" Xerxes smirked, leaning cavalierly upon his pillow. "Go now!"

Mehuman glanced at his fellow eunuchs, his face full of doubt.

But, failing to dissuade the king, and knowing that he dare not try again, he bowed and left the chamber.

The other six eunuchs did likewise; following their master, they scrambled for the hall.

"Can he mean it?" Abagtha marveled.

"He means it," Mehuman sighed. "And we shall comply, though I fear going before the queen with this request more than I fear defying the king."

10

With nearly as much expense and finery, Vashti had entertained the ladies of the kingdom since the beginning of the year. This final week, she, like her husband, designated the celebration for the palace workers as well as for the wives, daughters, sisters, mothers, and grandmothers of the men who reveled in Xerxes' court.

But her banquet and her festivities were of a different sort than the wild abandon which characterized the men's party.

The ladies feasted on the daintiest of foods, the rarest of wines. But the temperament of the women's garden was marked with ladylike restraint.

The displays which the queen paraded for their viewing pleasure were not calculated to inflate their estimation of her own glory or wealth. She had scheduled dancers and musicians as well as jugglers and clowns and acrobats, just as had Xerxes, but their acts did not appeal to prurient interests and the occasional fashion show which edged the court was not a display of the queen's own garments and jewels but had been put together by experts who wished to show the latest in womanly attire for the interest and entertainment of the guests.

None of what Vashti presented was intended to arouse jealousy or to pique her own pride.

Nor would her guests dream of humiliating this sovereign lady by drinking to excess or by gormandizing on the delicacies she provided. Often she encouraged them to display their own talents, inviting this one to sing for the group or that one to tell a fetching story.

All in all, the scene in Vashti's court was a far cry in color and demeanor from that promulgated by her husband.

And the queen enjoyed it immensely. If any heavy thought tinged her pleasure, it was the realization that Xerxes had changed, the knowledge that what went on in his pavilion would have embarrassed herself and her guests had they been privy to it.

Just now she strolled with several of her companions along an arbor path, the scent of hyacinths and roses making a heady climax to a satisfying evening. Several hundred women lounged around the fountains of her retreat, listening to the entrancing notes of a flute and observing the fluid movements of a young dancer decked in trailing scarves. Surges of soft applause brought a smile to Vashti's lips as she conversed amiably with her closest friends, wives of prominent noblemen, daughters of the seven highest houses in the land, and sisters of her childhood.

When a slave came running, announcing the appearance at the garden door of Xerxes' eunuchs, Vashti was not a little surprised.

"They say they have a request for you, from His Highness, your husband," the messenger explained.

The queen's face lit with enthusiasm. It must be, she reasoned, that Xerxes wished to meet her after his grand celebration for a private rendezvous.

When she went to the door to receive the eunuchs, therefore, she was troubled to see their uneasy countenances.

"Your Majesty, live forever!" Mehuman cried, falling on his face before Vashti. The other valets, likewise bowed themselves to the floor, and when the queen asked them to rise, Mehuman's face was red.

"Queen Vashti," he stammered, "Our Lord Xerxes wishes us to convey an invitation . . ."

"Yes?" the woman spurred him.

"He wishes you to come before him . . ."

Aha, she had supposed right! He wished to have her private company this night.

". . . with the royal crown upon your head . . ."

The queen studied Mehuman in amazement. She never wore the heavy ornament except to make public appearances.

"Go on," she whispered.

". . . so that he might show you to his companions."

Vashti, scarcely believing her ears, surveyed the man with contempt.

"Say again," she commanded.

Mehuman summoned as much diplomacy as he could muster, and cleared his throat. "He wishes to bestow upon his friends the gift of your beauty, My Queen. He would have you appear before his servants and noblemen, that they may . . . gaze upon you."

The eunuch sighed. Try as he might, there was no graceful way to dispense with this duty. And when the royal lady evinced incredulity, her poise a poor covering for utter horror, he looked away shamefaced.

At this pronouncement Vashti's lady friends began to mutter among themselves, and quickly their astonishment caught the attention of others in the court, until the entire company of guests grew apprehensive.

The music ceased, the dancer stopped in her steps, and silence descended.

No queen of Persia had ever been placed in such a predicament. No matter how Vashti responded, her integrity was at stake.

It was beyond comprehension that a royal spouse would ever defy a king. Yet it was also inconceivable that a regal lady should expose herself to a crowd of drunken, leering males, be they friends of her husband or gutter vagabonds.

A queen was expected to be the epitome of wifely duty and purity. What she chose to do spoke to all women of the realm, and were she to disobey her lord and master, her actions could easily be misconstrued as condoning the undermining of male authority everywhere.

Indeed, Vashti was in a most uncomfortable and irresolvable dilemma.

The silence burned her ears as the scrutinizing gaze of a thousand eyes seared her back.

As she looked upon the man with the bowed head, time seemed to stand still. Her next words could mean life or death to her. Were she to actually refuse the king's invitation, she could lose everything.

Memories of Xerxes' coolness toward her, of his unthinking rejections over recent months, still haunted her. And she had no way of knowing just how cruel he might be if she were to resist his summons.

Yet it was a certainty that an appearance before the inebriated mob in his court would forever mar her own selfhood, stripping her of a dignity even more precious than Xerxes' esteem.

"Tell the king I shall *not* appear," she replied.

A rush of whispers and a rattle of shaking heads and conferring voices followed her words.

Some denied that she had said what she did. Others insisted that she had.

Mehuman himself, who had heard the words directly, trembled with wonder.

"Your Majesty?" he marveled.

"Tell the king I shall *not* appear," Vashti repeated.

Indeed, she *had* chosen disobedience! Like a flurry of chortling doves, a chorus of awe-filled commentary rose through the roofless air.

Gathering her silken robes in calm hands, Vashti departed the garden, her head held high, her back straight as an upright spear.

11

"She what?" Xerxes growled, leaping from his couch of pleasure and glowering at Mehuman.

Despite the loud partying which went on in the court below,
guests turned in surprise at this sudden movement on the king's
part.

Only the seven eunuchs knew the reason for his volcanic
reaction. Only Mehuman and his cohorts knew of the ludicrous
summons sent to Vashti.

"The queen refuses to appear," the chief valet repeated,
cringing as though he himself might receive the full force of the
king's anger.

Indeed, such a thing was not out of the question.

Messengers had been known to die at the whim of a dissat-
isfied monarch for bearing less sorry news than this.

Xerxes' fury pushed past his drunken lethargy, pulsating in
clenched fists and throbbing temples. Face red, the emperor
paced to and fro before his couch until every eye in the room was
on him and not a sound of music, laughter, or even of breathing
broke the air.

The eunuchs to Mehuman's back stood with bowed heads,
cowering together like a pack of desert dogs, fearing that their
fate, like Mehuman's, hung in the balance.

Meanwhile, seven other fellows, the king's legal counselors,
began to draw near. Thinking that there must be some matter of
politics, injustice, or threat against their master, they were eager
to assist him.

"Your Majesty," their leader intervened, "what troubles you?
May we help in any way?"

Xerxes, too flustered and wine-soaked to readily reply, only continued to pace his porch. At last Mehuman answered for him.

"Our Lord sent a summons to his queen, requesting that she appear at his party . . . so that all of the men might . . . gaze upon her."

Mehuman's own embarrassment was evident, though he tried to conceal it. And the attorney, Memucan, was caught in a hard place.

Not quite as inebriated as the emperor, he instantly understood the queen's reticence to comply. But at the same time he knew he dare not call the king's commandment into question.

Looking awkwardly at his fellow lawyers, he sought some suggestion, but they only shrugged, not wishing to touch the matter.

However, it was too late to withdraw an offer of assistance. And when Xerxes turned to them, his bloodshot eyes full of ire, it was their turn to cringe.

"So what shall we do about this situation?" the emperor demanded. "What penalty does the law provide for a queen who refuses to obey the king's orders, properly sent through his aides?"

Again Memucan looked to his fellow counselors. Did the emperor want an honest answer? In his drunken state, did he have any idea what he was asking?

The drama was now open to a thousand observers. What was decided here today would play heavily upon families throughout the empire. Most important to those present, it would play on the image of the king and the status of men throughout the realm.

Surely, were Xerxes in a more rational condition, matters would not have gone this far. Nevertheless, it was Memucan's responsibility to handle the king's legal affairs. Though this time he was not dealing in matters of criminal justice or interprovincial legislation, he had been asked a direct question. And it concerned issues perhaps equally as great as ones of imperial policy.

Shuffling uneasily, he fumbled for a reply. In truth, there was no specific injunction regarding this dilemma, and no precedent in Persian history, for no queen had ever thus defied her husband.

Naturally, uppermost in the counselors' minds was their own welfare. The advice they framed must appease the king's anger and bring them the best advantage.

Noting his retributive countenance, they knew that no soft action would suffice to save his pride. Vashti could be reprimanded and undergo some loss of privilege, but what if she were to disobey him in the future on some other matter? Surely the attorneys would pay dearly for not recommending a stiffer penalty. Furthermore, they were aware of the careful scrutiny which their advice would receive from other noblemen of the realm. If it were too gentle, it could appear to favor the undermining of men's authority in general.

Therefore, looking to their own futures, it was clear that their decision and their counsel must take a hard line.

They discussed this only briefly among themselves. All of them saw the implications of mercy all too well, and therefore their conference was brief.

While the emperor still paced his deck, wringing his hands and scowling at the courtiers who lined the walls, Memucan addressed his question adroitly.

"Your Majesty, live forever," he said, bowing before Xerxes. "My friends and I have considered the crime and have reached a conclusion."

"Speak!" the monarch bellowed, weary of delay.

"Queen Vashti has wronged not only the king, but every official and citizen of your empire. For women everywhere will begin to disobey their husbands when they learn what Queen Vashti has done."

At this a murmur of agreement arose from the besotted crowd, and so Memucan took courage.

"Before this day is out, the wife of every one of us will hear what the queen did and will begin to deal with her husband in like manner. There will be contempt throughout your realm."

Again a chorus of consensus rang from the court, and Memucan began to swagger with confidence.

"Therefore," he declared, "we suggest that, subject to your agreement, you issue a royal edict, a law of the Medes and Persians that can never be revoked, that Queen Vashti be forever banished from your presence and that you choose another queen more worthy than she! When this decree is published throughout your great kingdom, husbands everywhere, whatever their rank, will be respected by their wives!"

Because Memucan was more aware at this moment of the reaction of the crowd than of the king, he swelled with glory. He did not note the emperor's sudden halt, nor did the twinge of grief which passed over Xerxes' face reach his inflated spirit.

Few, in fact, heeded the monarch's mood, so taken were they with Memucan's daring.

Perhaps the valets, intimately acquainted as they were with their master, thought they read a less-than-enthusiastic expression on his face. But not one of them encouraged a rebuttal, fearing the authority of the counselors.

Of course, Memucan's advice was founded on the most bizarre logic. That every wife in the realm would begin to despise her husband based on Vashti's actions was pure paranoia, and that the crowd could embrace such an assumption was classic evidence of their alcohol-altered mentality.

But then, such was the mood of taverns late at night, the coveys of negligence and excess where men supported one another and where women were warned against. Such was the potential reasoning wherever wayward husbands gathered, and wherever families were scorned by guilt-ridden souls.

All of this might be clear in the light of day, when the haze of alcohol lifted and the clarity of sober thinking descended. But it was not clear now, and *now* was when the decision would be made.

Xerxes, though appalled by the advice, would never admit it under these circumstances. Though he could see its folly, even through besotted eyes, he could not speak against it before a thousand comrades.

He was a man, a man's man, a man of men. To soften now, even for the sake of Vashti, his "most treasured possession," was unthinkable.

As the company in the court looked to him for his reaction to the attorney's counsel, his face was a mask of unwavering strength. Behind it was the soul of a young boy, the one who had once stood with Vashti upon her father's balcony, who had promised always to cherish her, who had reveled in her love and thrilled to her caress. But the mask would win tonight, the love of men's approval, the insecurity which drove him always to conquest.

Hesitating only briefly, he looked at his valets, at the counselors, and at his many assistants. Not one gave argument against Memucan, and each, when pressed, colluded in the deception that he agreed, giving assent with a nod.

"Let it be," Xerxes said, his voice huskier than he wished.

And with this he turned for his private chamber for the comfort of another wine goblet and for the sanctuary of sleep.

12

As morning sun filtered past the heavy blinds of Xerxes' chamber, he rolled over with an ache in his chest. His head throbbed after days and nights of drinking. But the dull pain in his heart was more troubling than the hangover.

At first, as he struggled to sit erect, propping himself against his pillows, he could not recall why he should feel such heaviness. But as wakefulness replaced drugged stupor, recollection pierced him like a physician's scalpel.

"Vashti!" he groaned, staggering from his bed.

He was alone with the dim reality of what he had done the night before. As it settled over him in waves of irrefutable certainty, as the growing illumination that it was no dream, no nightmare, crashed in upon him, the ache in his breast brought tears to his eyes.

Limping to the window, he pulled back the curtain and stared into a high-noon desert. He had slept too long. His commandment would already have been fulfilled, and Vashti would have long ago been shunted from the palace.

Exiles of Persia could be sent to any number of wild and isolated places. In his besotted condition the night before he had made no formal selection of a site for her banishment, and he knew now that her fate had been left to the whim of whoever hauled her away.

"Almighty Ahura-Mazda!" he cried, falling to his knees. The bleak wilderness of the uncharted Zagros haunted him, beckoning with blunted fingers across miles of steamy mirage. "Where is she? Where is my beloved?"

But there was no retracting his judgment. There was no

reversing his command.

The one who had waited for his attentions night after night would wait no longer. For she could never be his again.

ESTHER

PART III
Descent of a Kingdom

13

Hadassah stood outside the village gate, gazing across the swaying grainfields. It neared sunset, and she knew that her cousin David would soon be returning from his daylong labor of scything ripe barley into sheaf-ready piles. She would wait here in the harvest gloaming, enveloped in twilight until he returned.

The sickles of a hundred workers had raised a fine dust through the evening air. The sun's setting was therefore a crimson blush, billows of coral clouds reflecting the same color that sailors see when they watch the golden orb descend through a veil of fog.

But there was no sea here—only endless miles of hot earth, fertile in the Zagros valley, but nevertheless a desert.

As Hadassah watched the returning laborers, their sweat-streaked bodies glistening in the pink light, many of them nodded to her, passing through the small town gate with words of greeting. No man among them failed to appreciate the fresh beauty of the teenaged girl, and it was safe to say that each bore a bit of envy for David, knowing that it was he who held her heart.

"He is not far behind," one elderly fellow acknowledged, smiling as she blushed and looked away. As soon as he was gone, however, she was on tiptoe, seeking the figure of her cousin in the suspended haze.

When at last she spied him, one of the very last to arrive, her heart stirred eagerly, though not without a twinge of sadness. Too often she read growing frustration in David's face. Eighteen he was, and bound forever, it seemed, to work the soil. His artist's soul had not died, though at times he surely wished it would so that he might find contentment with his lot and not continually wish for broader opportunities.

It had not escaped her, however, that when David was with her, the sadness lifted. Such was the case just now, as, coming upon her, his countenance lightened and a smile touched his lips.

Though Hadassah knew he resented his lot, she always considered him most beautiful when he returned from the fields. Always he was her golden boy, gold of hair and eyes, but never more than when he had put in a day beneath the sun, his skin bronzed and the fine chaffy silt of harvest clinging to his torso.

"Hello, Blossom," he greeted, lifting his heavy scythe higher on his shoulder, his free arm scooping her into a playful embrace. The term was one of endearment, playing with the meaning of her name, "Myrtle." As much as David was her goldpiece, she was his priceless flower. And though neither of them had ever revealed in words the depth of their caring, every action and every expression betrayed it.

"Cousin Leah says supper will be ready any moment," Hadassah said, laughing as he hugged her.

"We will be there in time," he replied. "Sit with me a while."

Drawing her aside, he guided her to a grove of gnarled palms which shaded a corner of the town wall and bade her rest with him in the little oasis.

"But aren't you very hungry?" she marveled, knowing that he usually rushed home for dinner like a starving prodigal.

"I am," he agreed, "and thirsty." At this he pulled from his belt a skin-bottle of warm wine and swigged it eagerly. Capping it, he sighed, "But I have not seen you for days. That is more important."

Hadassah had not visited the village for several weeks, for her papa was busy with the inventory of Vashti's abandoned possessions, stored in the queen's warehouse during this full year since her banishment.

It was a sad task, one put off all these months since her going, in deference to the king's wishes.

"I suppose the queen's inventory *could* take a while to count," David smirked, showing his disdain for the royal household.

"Yes," Hadassah nodded. "But Vashti was a good queen," she insisted. "A very good woman."

David noted the defensiveness that Hadassah always manifested when she spoke of the grand lady. Many times she had recounted the occasion when she observed Vashti's kindness firsthand. It had made a lasting impression upon her young mind, and David knew she admired the queen's refusal to accommodate the drunken king.

Mordecai had not been present at the banquet when Vashti was deposed, having attended during an earlier shift. But in his growing love of Judaism and skepticism of Persian politics he conceded that Jehovah would have honored Vashti's choice, and that her exile was a crime for which Xerxes would pay dearly.

"Where do you suppose she is?" Hadassah sighed, gazing wistfully across the desert.

David, sensitive to her tender feelings, knew the question reflected sincere concern for her heroine.

"I have heard there is a great highway," he replied, "running all the way to India—the silk route, plied by kingly caravans and fabled merchants. Have you heard this?"

"Yes," Hadassah answered, warming to the poetry in David's speech.

His eyes took on a faraway look, and she knew he pondered not just the queen's fate but also the many distant places which he could visit only in daydreams.

"She could have been taken that direction, to any of a hundred outposts along the way. Or," he continued, studying the bleak range which hemmed the valley, "it is said that years ago the royal house sent Greeks into the Zagros, captives taken by Darius when he passed into Europe. Perhaps the queen was sent to dwell with them."

Despite the heat Hadassah shivered, considering the irony of such a possibility. "But Xerxes plans war on the Greeks," she objected. "Surely he would not send his wife to live with the enemies."

David smiled fondly at the girl. "Can you think of a better punishment?" he asked.

Hadassah kicked absently at the dirt. "What a dreadful man the king must be!" she exclaimed, her face contorted with anger.

But David, wishing to lighten her mood, drew nearer, directing her to study the vast valley floor.

"On the other hand, "he offered, "perhaps she plays with the Quasqui."

"The Quasqui?" she repeated.

"Nomads of the plain," he said. "I saw them once when I was a small boy. My Papa took me on a trip to Ecbatana and we saw their encampment one evening, near the oasis where we slept."

His romantic soul surged at the memory, and he pulled Hadassah close as he recounted it.

"They live like kings in their own right, you know—summer homes and winter homes, mountains in the heat, valley in the cold. And they eat like kings, on roast wild partridge and grilled lamb livers, wafer-thin bread and fragrant tea, yogurt and skewered quail. They sleep on downy quilts and sing to guitars . . ."

Hadassah was breathless as he wove these images, entranced as much by his mesmerizing voice as by the word pictures he painted.

"I heard them sing a love song that night while they were camped about their fire. Beautiful it was!" he declared, taking Hadassah's hand in his.

" 'The tribe has left, the dust remains,' " he sang, his voice liquid and mellow. " 'The sun has gone, the yellow glow remains; I never kissed those dark eyes . . . the sorrow remains . . .' "

As he recited the last phrase, he gazed into the girl's open countenance with a strange sorrow, a sadness for which she could not account.

And her fingers trembled in his grip.

The sun was sinking fast, dark coming upon them all too quickly. Eyes closed, Hadassah tilted her head back. For a long moment David studied her supple lips, but then he suddenly stood, pulling her to him and bending over her with a hesitant sigh.

"We must be going now," he whispered, resisting the urge to kiss her. Turning, he led her back to the village.

After all, he told himself, she was a child of status and he was but a poor farmer. He thought it best not to love her.

14

Xerxes had spent four years preparing for his invasion of Greece. Shipbuilding alone had taken nearly a quarter of the imperial budget.

One thousand seaworthy vessels were launched from the eastern shore of the Mediterranean and the north shore of Africa when at last he went to war. His forces, the most numerous ever to traipse the earth, were led by his three brothers, the sons of Darius with whom he had dreamed his greatest dreams since childhood.

Arsames was placed in charge of an enormous Ethiopian contingent, and Achaemenes and Anatrigines shared the leadership of the navy. As for Xerxes himself, he took the admiralty of the Phoenician fleet, fulfilling an ambitious vision for a man reared in Persia's landlocked interior.

This afternoon a balmy breeze swelled the sails of his trireme as 600 oars pushed the sleek vessel across the Thracian Sea toward the Greek mainland. He had traveled by camelback up the royal Persian highway from Susa through the Taurus Range, and after entering the Cicilian Gates he had crossed the Hellespont by two bridges of boats. Awaiting Xerxes in the Greek towns of Asia Minor (which his father, Darius, had conquered a dozen years before) had been standing armies levied for his purposes against their European compatriots. He had enlisted some of them as sailors and had left the rest to his generals for invasion against the Hellespont's western shore.

Darius, more bent on reconstruction than revenge, had established democracies in the Ionian towns. Therefore it was with mixed feelings that the Greek forces met the emperor, some of them grateful to Persia for its fair treatment but others, especially the older ones, still full of resentment against their conquerors.

Xerxes had spent the winter at Sardis before advancing on Ionia. Ahead of him he had sent supplies, and now stores of corn for his infantry were accumulated at intervals leading all the way into Europe.

In all, nearly two million foot soldiers and sailors composed the force that Xerxes brought with him from Mesopotamia and points east. As they were joined by contingents from about the empire, he would be advancing upon Europe with over five million men, the most awesome horde ever to practice battle.

His dream this day as he stood at the helm of the warship, observing the pilot's dexterous work and listening to the chanting slap of the vessel's oars, was that all the West would be his. As the sleek bark passed island after island along the Dolopes chain, his pulse skipped.

This was, he reasoned, where a man's heart ought to be: in war and its implements, in power and command. Nothing short of this was worthy of attention, and surely not of grief.

Vashti should have come to him when he called for her. Did she not know that matters of marriage and love could not always be of grand importance? Not to a king, anyway.

In the cold heights of the Asian mountains, as he had slept in his guarded tent, he had often reminded himself of this. On desert nights when he slept beside his spear, and wondered where Vashti was, he had taken comfort in the conviction that such questions were beneath him.

As he had ridden high in his camel's swaying canopy, leading his millions toward the goal of glory, he had forced his queen from his mind, drugged by the call of destiny and the praise of his comrades.

In time, he told himself, she would cease to haunt him. When he owned Europe and held the entire world in his grip, she would fade forever from memory.

Just now, scanning the advancing shore, the coast which cradled Athens and Sparta, he girded his spirit for adventure—adventure craved by his forefathers but never tasted.

Where Xerxes set foot, Persia set foot. As Persia prospered, so would his soul.

This he told himself when Vashti's sweet face darted across his conscience. It worked to quell his guilt, to appease his yearning for her touch—sometimes.

15

For several months Xerxes' millions had been positioned at various sites throughout the Aegean and Thracian Seas. When 180,000 of them went against the Athens-Sparta alliance, they were met by only 10,000 Greeks and 300 ships.

On their way to Athens the Persians had encountered unprecedented victory at Thermopylae. When they easily overtook the Greek capital, besieging the acropolis and setting the temple of Athena aflame, the horrified Athenians bowed to eastern occupation with chagrin.

For the first time in history an Oriental power not only invaded the West but held its most prestigious city in a stranglehold. Xerxes had, therefore, fulfilled more of the Persian expansionist dream than any of his predecessors, and after sending word of victory to Susa he headed for Salamis, plotting to take over the entire Dorian sector of the Hellenistic world.

It was September 23, over a year into the emperor's European experience. What he had only imagined in fantasy was spread before him as he sat beneath a striped umbrella high atop a hill at the head of Piraeus Harbor. A soft southern breeze wafted up from the Myrtoum Sea, bringing the scent of clashing steel and the sound of bloody cries across Salamis Isle.

This was the gateway to all points west. If Xerxes won this round, nothing could stand in his way. Though the forces were fairly equal, the Persians, having demoralized the Greeks at Athens, were enjoying the advantage.

Xerxes straightened the silken folds of his lavender gown and rested his flared sleeves upon the arms of his portable throne. Sunshine glinted off his upturned face as his secretaries raced back and forth with word of his captains' exploits. Dozens of

ships representing both sides of the fray expressed their differ-
ences in the narrow slit of water separating Salamis from the
mainland. While presently the battle was quite balanced, the
emperor was confident.

His Phoenician navy was an awesome contingent, not only for
expertise but also for appearance. Its squat, flat-bottomed boats,
propelled by two decks of oars, denoted divine retribution with
their huge idols of the stocky god, Baal, leaning threateningly
from each prow and with sharp-nosed battering rams pushing
ominously through the water.

The Greeks' more curvaceous, streamlined vessels appeared
fragile by comparison, and although the goddess Athena was
often depicted as a warrior, in crested helmet and full armor, her
likeness did not adorn her ships.

Despite the huskiness of the Phoenician craft, however, the
Greek ships proved themselves a formidable force. About dusk
the scales began to tip in favor of the Europeans, and Xerxes'
secretaries hesitated to bear the discomforting tidings to their
king.

Nevertheless, it was increasingly apparent that, while the
Phoenicians were masters of the open seas, the more slender and
maneuverable Greek barks were better able to cope with the
restricting canal. The Hellenists, accustomed to the narrow
shoals and treacherous conditions of island waterways, managed
to lure the Phoenicians into straits beyond their ken.

Perhaps Xerxes need not be told the worst. He could surely
see for himself the broken wreckage of several Persian vessels floating in the canal. And along the rocky shore wounded
sailors swam, clambering up the beach toward the village of
Psyttaleia.

Soon, from the vantage point of his sheltered throne, Xerxes
could see that nearly the entire Persian garrison scrambled
ashore, thousands upon thousands abandoning floundered
ships and dragging wounded comrades across bloody sands.

Close on their heels followed the enemy, shooting down those
who ran and falling upon the disabled as they hacked them to
pieces with broadaxes.

Those still manning the faltering ships retreated now, trying
to flee the scene of battle, the waters strewn with hulks and

corpses and flailing swimmers. Few would escape, taking with them the memory of comrades clubbed to death by the enemy's oars or spitted like tunny on steamy lances.

The slaughter continued until nightfall. Two hundred Persian ships were lost in the Salamis strait to only 40 Greek vessels. While the emperor's fugitives fled to Phalerum, the chagrined monarch sat like a statue upon his regal chair.

As the sun dipped over the westland, which he still longed to possess, tears trickled down his cheeks. And a Mediterranean breeze, warm but not conciliatory, dried them.

*   *   *

Winter was approaching. Xerxes and his defeated troops limped back to Susa along the same route they had followed into Europe.

Though he was not utterly abandoning dreams of westward expansion, the emperor must give his demoralized and disorganized forces time to recuperate. Those who retreated with him would be sent home, most of them too badly wounded to fight again. The larger part of his army, that which had not seen action at Salamis, had been sent north to await spring. Under General Mardonius they would seek alliance with Athens, and though Xerxes had lost command of the sea, a fleet now guarded the Hellespont, plotting another foray into the hinterland.

The dream was tentative, however. As Xerxes withdrew into Asia, word came from other parts of Greece that his brothers, all three of them top commanders, had given their lives in his cause.

How swiftly ambition had turned to ashes, dreams to dust! Somewhere in the foothills of Cicilia, Xerxes laid his royal head upon a lonely pillow and remembered Persepolis, the ceremonial halls where he and his young brothers had been trained for war.

Little was left to him now of human love. Father, wife, and kin were gone. Only the adoration of his subjects remained, and unless he took the West, even that hollow consolation could fade away.

16

Xerxes, Emperor of the East, trembled as he knelt in his private chapel before the frieze of his god, Ahura-Mazda. In stone relief the winged deity hovered above him, its wheeled craft soaring, aloof, yet unmoving.

For weeks all of Susa had sat on edge as news from Greece fluctuated between victory and defeat.

Mardonius, left with the best of Xerxes' troops to complete the work begun in Attica, had failed to achieve an alliance with the trampled Athenians, and so had occupied the city since spring. Recent word was that the Greeks had at last taken the offensive, and so the general had burned the capital to the ground, thus procuring an empty retribution by destroying the greatest prize of the emperor's campaign and evacuating Attica itself.

While there was strong Persian fighting here and there throughout the Greek isles, just today a messenger had brought tidings that Mardonius and his troops were huddled behind a wall of felled trees at Plataea, and that their situation was very precarious.

Nearly a full year had passed since the battle of Salamis. In all this time Xerxes had slept little, eaten little, and fretted much, living only for the sporadic reports which filtered to his palace from the warfront.

The three battle points which counted most were at Plataea, Mycale, and Sestos. If Mardonius lost Plataea, one-third of Xerxes' remaining hope would die. And so he prayed today in the small sanctuary adjoining his bedchamber—pleading with his god to give his generals wisdom, his admirals craftiness, and his armed men strength.

Every day of his life he had practiced prayer, but the last time he had done so with such determination was when he begged

Ahura-Mazda to hasten his wedding to Vashti. The god had granted that request. Perhaps he would grant this one.

But as Xerxes knelt before the carving of his beloved deity, he doubted whether his petition would be honored. Fasting and agonizing until his face was gaunt and lined, he wondered if the god who had blessed him with the girl of his dreams could ever again look kindly upon him after he had sent her away.

Soon enough his doubts were confirmed. A rap upon the chapel door lifted him from his knees.

"Enter," he called hoarsely.

Pushing open the door, the chamberlain admitted three young boys, all dusty and windblown, having traveled hundreds of miles and each bearing word from the European forces.

Quickly the news was dispensed as the youngsters fawned and shivered before the mightiest man on earth. Mardonius and his troops had been slaughtered like sheep at Plataea, the fleet at Mycale had been destroyed, and the garrison at Sestos, being reduced to eating their bedstraps, had abandoned the town by night.

Xerxes, receiving the messages numbly, could have called for the execution of the three lads. Instead, after gazing upon them mutely, he dismissed them and turned again to his prayers.

"Mighty Ahura-Mazda, you who answer when I call, *so* you have answered," he wept.

Burying his nails in his scalp, he mourned—for himself as well as for those who had given everything for him.

17

The seven eunuchs—Mehuman, Biztha, Harbona, Bigtha, Abagtha, Zethar, and Carkas—stood outside the king's council chamber, peering past his guards and consulting among themselves.

"For days he has sat thus," Mehuman whispered, his face furrowed with concern. "He mutters to himself a great deal, and whispers Vashti's name too often."

The eunuchs studied the king's slumped form as he rested upon his throne, and they shook their heads sadly.

"It is not only his defeat in Europe which haunts him," Biztha surmised.

"I think it is less that than anything," Mehuman agreed. "He shall rally from that in time, for there are always more lands to conquer. But Vashti he shall never forget."

"It is our responsibility to lift His Majesty's spirits," Zethar announced, his chin jutting in determination. "We must think of something!"

The others murmured agreement, and through a process of elimination they began to arrive at a plan.

"Riches are not the answer. We should make no suggestion which could inflate his coffers," Carkas reasoned.

"Right," nodded Abagtha, "nor would a round of parties or entertainers do the trick."

"I agree," said Harbona. "And we have already ruled out conquest."

Bigtha shrugged. "A *woman* has been his downfall; perhaps a woman can *save* him!"

All eyes were on Mehuman, awaiting his response to this astute observation.

For a long moment he contemplated the matter. Then a smile tugged at his lips.

"Very well," he assented. "I can see no other way. We must provide the king with a romance, something to surpass what he had with Vashti."

The others nodded enthusiastically. But then, one by one, their faces fell.

"How can such a thing be accomplished?" Carkas stammered. "His love for Vashti was a rare thing. And there are no women from among the seven royal families to compare with her."

Carkas' referred to the injunction that no queen was to be taken from outside the seven highest houses in Persia, a law established by Darius in order to honor the seven men who had been loyal to him during an insurrection.

"This is true," Mehuman conceded. "But our king's health is failing. Something must be done. And this law was made years ago. It is reversible under a new administration."

The eunuchs raised their eyebrows at this, but would not question Mehuman's interpretation of the edict. Indeed, there was no formal stipulation regarding an emperor's contradicting the decisions of a former ruler.

"Still," Carkas objected, "where are we to find a woman worthy of Xerxes?"

Biztha jumped on this. "Why, we should seek high and low for her. We should bring beauties from all about the king's empire, and let him choose for himself!"

At first the suggestion seemed so absurd that the others laughed—all except Mehuman. And when he seemed to be thinking upon it, the snickers subsided.

"You cannot actually take such a notion seriously!" Harbona cried. "Why, this is tantamount to calling for a new harem— something Xerxes would never condone. Did he not just recently divest himself of such pleasures, sending hundreds of women from the palace?"

Mehuman did not reply quickly, but peered in at the king, who sat lethargically in his solemn chamber, tipping a goblet of red wine back and forth and gazing upon its contents.

"A man in His Majesty's condition could consider almost anything," he concluded. "Give him a few more days, and then we shall approach him."

18

Hadassah sat up in bed and peered toward the dim yellow light glowing beneath her chamber door. In rooms down the hall her female cousins, Marta and Isha, breathed in contented sleep beside their husbands. But voices in the parlor had jolted her awake.

Anxiously she leaned over the edge of her low pallet and tried to make out the words of Mordecai, Leah, and Moshe in the room beyond.

At first she could not believe her ears when she heard Mordecai in the house. He had not intended to come to the village until later in the season, giving her several more weeks of her seventeenth autumn to spend with her dearest companions. Why he should be here now, and in the middle of the night, she could not imagine. But she was not eager to return home. As much as she loved her adopted father, she much preferred to be with her cousins . . . especially with David.

As she pieced together snatches of the conversation, however, it seemed that Mordecai had not come to fetch her home, but was instead enlisting his sister's aid to continue maintaining her here.

Past a sleepy haze now, she managed to pick up the idea that some news from the palace greatly troubled her papa. As she concentrated on fragments of his story, she realized that he feared for her safety.

"'Let there be fair young virgins sought for the king,'" she heard him expostulate, as though he quoted some royal edict. "Can you believe that Xerxes would stoop to such indulgence?"

Leah's voice followed this, with a heavy sigh. "Well, though he has been known in the past as a moral man, Brother, he *is* a pagan, after all. He does not worship Jehovah. And remember that even certain of Israel's own kings kept harems—David . . . Solomon . . ."

"Yes," Mordecai granted. Despite his growing love of Judaism, he could be embarrassed by certain aspects of its history. "Still, it is disillusioning."

"Only if you expected better things," Moshe shrugged.

"So, go on," Leah urged him. "Surely you have come here at such an hour with more than courtroom gossip."

"I have," Mordecai acknowledged, rubbing his hands together anxiously. "Word in the palace is that the king has appointed officers in all the provinces to seek out and bring to Susa hundreds of young damsels. From among them, Xerxes shall choose a queen to replace his lost Vashti."

His eyes were wide as he spoke, and when his relations only studied him impersonally, he shook his head in frustration.

"Can't you see what this could mean? Are you blind, or am I the only one who has noticed my daughter's beauty?"

Suddenly, with a pang of recognition, Leah's breath came sharply.

"Hadassah!" she groaned, glancing toward the girl's chamber.

Her motherly heart raced protectively. Though there were other lovely maidens in the village, she knew that Hadassah outshone them, and that any procurator sent here would snatch up the willowy lass with the raven curls.

Nor need Mordecai go into detail as to how the king would sort through the hundreds brought to him. Moshe, drawing his manly shoulders into an indignant square, imagined the sweet child herded into Xerxes' bedchamber, to be exploited and then tossed aside.

"What can we do?" he whispered, almost afraid that the sniffing hounds were in the street at this very moment.

Mordecai paced the floor of the tiny parlor. "You must try to keep her from daylight until this misery passes. She must remain with you, and you must keep her from view."

"But," Leah gasped, "how are we to explain this to Hadassah? Surely it would terrify her to know the truth."

"Indeed," Mordecai agreed. "She is very innocent about such things. A good girl, she is. You know?"

"Of course," Moshe assured him. "We know her as well as you do."

"Then," the guardian declared, "tell her whatever you must. But keep her secluded."

At this the voices tapered to a solemn whisper. Hadassah leaned back upon her pillow, her hands clutching at her blanket, and her whole body aquiver.

19

When the eunuchs had presented Xerxes with the proposed "solution" to his loneliness and depression, he had grasped at it. Of course, as at the party where he had deposed Vashti, his decision to seek a new queen had been made through a wine-soaked fog. There would be times throughout the ensuing months when he would feel the guilt of this choice, just as he felt remorse over the loss of his wife. But he would manage to push it aside as day after day lovelies were paraded before him.

It took only a few weeks, following his acceptance of the advice, for the harem quarters to be refurbished and for hand-picked virgins to begin arriving at the palace, first from points closest and then from provinces along the farthest reaches of the empire. Soon the king's manly blood was stirred by the presence of innocent beauty in his courts.

Access to the damsels would be postponed, however, for what became an excruciatingly long time as the girls were put through a routine of cleansing rituals and beautification, taking a full 12 months from the time of their arrival. The king's desire, piqued by this anticipation, began to alleviate his former depression, replacing it with energies he must release in creative ways.

Mehuman, the eunuch, had foreseen this. When Biztha had proposed the procurement of a new harem, he had quickly realized the effect that a bevy of women on the palace grounds would have upon the emperor. And as Xerxes began to take up administrative duties with a vengeance, channeling his aroused and unrequited passions into business, politics, and parties, the valet smiled with private gratification. "As good as a physician's prescription!" he reasoned. "Our king is himself again."

It was the month of Tebeth, "mud" month of midwinter, four

years after Vashti's deposition and more than a year since Xerxes' defeat at Salamis. Even in Susa, the weather was cold.

Hadassah worked in the smoky kitchen of Leah's little cottage, chatting gaily with her cousins. Her seclusion, which had begun three months before, did not seem so strange once the weather turned bad. Until the muddy time, Leah and Moshe had expected to be questioned often by their niece as to why they found so much for her to do inside and kept such close track of her whenever she went outdoors. But, to their surprise, she had accepted the peculiar isolation quietly, and had not once complained when Mordecai sent word that she should remain with them through the winter.

Though the guardians never suspected that the girl had overheard their midnight conversation with Mordecai, it was not long before news of the king's edict was public knowledge, and so Leah sought opportunity to caution the pretty girl.

Moshe, David, and the young husbands of Leah's two daughters were away from the house this evening, working beside the other men of the community to lay out fresh straw upon the empty grainfields, a duty required several times during the winter to prepare the muddy ground for spring planting.

The women labored over piles of onions and carrots in the dimly lit kitchen, peeling the vegetables for stews and soups. An aromatic broth simmered on the brick oven in the center of the room, and though it was chilly outside, the ladies wore light frocks in the steamy quarters.

Leah nervously broached the subject of the edict, addressing her daughters rather than Hadassah. "I hear there have been a good many coaches and carriages passing under the gates of Susa lately, bearing guests for the palace," she said.

"Guests?" Marta laughed. "Why, mother, you know all those young girls cannot be guests!"

Leah glanced at Hadassah, expecting her interest to be aroused. But the girl only kept her head bowed, intent upon the task of slicing cabbages.

"Well, then," the mother went on, "if we all know who the young ladies are, and why they have been taken to the palace . . ."

"Taken! Yes, Mother! They are *taken*, against their will, aren't they?" Isha cried. "How awful!"

"We are lucky we are married," Marta chimed in. "At least we needn't worry . . ." But then she caught herself, her hand flying to her mouth. "Oh, I am sorry," she groaned, gazing at Hadassah with round, sad eyes.

At this the girl at last looked up from her work, her own eyes moist with tears. Leah flew to Hadassah's side, throwing her arms about her.

"Dear child!" she wept, seeing unconcealed terror in the innocent face. "You have known all along, haven't you?"

The girl did not reply, but nestled her dark head upon her cousin's shoulder.

"Then I needn't warn you more strongly," Leah insisted, lifting Hadassah's chin and studying her perfect countenance. "You must be careful. Continue close to home. Do not go out in the daylight, or linger, as you often do, near the gate when David comes back from the fields. Do you hear me?"

"I hear you," Hadassah stammered, frightened all the more by Leah's curt tone.

Softening, the woman held her close and looked anxiously at her daughters. Drawing near, they embraced their cousin, and together the women stood in a huddle, listening to the wind outside and wishing their men would return.

20

The flame of the candle on the window ledge fluttered uneasily as a rainy breeze pushed through the half-open reed blind. Soon David, Moshe, and the other girls' husbands would be coming in from the fields. Surely, Hadassah reasoned, it could not hurt if she sat in the little hall of Leah's entryway and watched for them in the street outside.

This had always been a safe little hamlet. Folk did not cover their windows with grates or slats, as in the city. Only in inclement weather did they even lower flimsy shades like this one, which admitted the winter wind.

Feeling quite secure within the house, Hadassah rested her elbows upon the sill and leaned her chin on one hand. A slender moon glanced between heavy clouds, and she remembered the night that she and David had sat in the little oasis beyond the town wall.

She was of marriageable age, and had never met a man more to her liking than David. Having lived much of her life in the royal city, she had seen many a handsome and wealthy fellow. But David was a kindred soul.

A good man he was—committed to his family despite the fact that such service frustrated his desires to pursue his artistic leanings. Yet he did find ways, even in the village, to express the creative side of himself. Many a night he sat beside the parlor fire, spinning glorious yarns in song and poem, of mountains, bedouins, and distant kingdoms. When a spare moment granted the luxury, he painted or carved his imaginings upon small shards of pottery and hunks of cast-off alabaster.

From the parlor, the orange glow of Leah's little firepit blended with the flame of Hadassah's window candle. Trickles of gentle rain dashed against the sill, and her mind drifted out toward the fields, toward the one she loved.

A stir down the street seemed to say that the men were coming in from the evening's labors. Eager voices from many doorways called out greetings.

Hadassah leaned her head out the window, straining for the sight of David rounding the dark streetcorner.

The flash of torches verified that a company passed into town. Had she not been anticipating her cousin, she might have paid more attention to the accompanying sounds, for housewifely hellos were suddenly muffled, and cries and weeping followed.

Too soon for her preoccupied heart to heed this change, the approaching torchlight blazed rudely across the housefront. Before she could duck inside, the disconcerting glare revealed faces unfamiliar to her. As though made to seek her out especially, one of the flares was brandished in her direction, lighting up her countenance like a miner's torch.

"Aha!" someone laughed. "Here's a pretty one!"

And then other voices joined in as Hadassah shielded her eyes.

"Pretty, indeed! She's a beauty!"

Lurching backward, Hadassah grappled with the blind.

But it was too late.

Leah came running from the kitchen just as the front door was kicked open and strong men in hard leather armor forced their way inside.

"This is your daughter?" the leader asked, grasping Hadassah by the arm.

"Why, no . . . yes . . ." Leah fumbled.

"Whatever," the official shrugged. "She now belongs to King Xerxes."

Crazed, the girl shrieked, and Leah clung to her until the guards beat her away.

Into the street Hadassah was thrown, her lavender dress torn at the shoulder and her pale face spattered with muddy rain.

Marta and Isha shrieked with her, holding onto one another as their favorite childhood playmate was thrust upon a waiting horse, and the horse was whipped into a gallop.

As the throng of thieving soldiers raced back toward the town gate, they took with them half a dozen girls of the village.

But the leader of the pack kept a keen eye on Hadassah. She was the evening's prize—perhaps the prize of his career.

He had done himself proud tonight.

21

Morning sun gleamed through a dreary blanket of fog over the palace of Susa. Mordecai the Jew sat in the gate of the royal house, behind his accounting table, and tried to keep his mind on the business of figures and ledgers.

On most days such preoccupation came easily to him despite the traffic of executives and officers who came and went upon the spacious stairway from the avenue out front. He was accustomed to the klatches of conversing courtiers and servants in the shady recesses of the gate's multistoried complex. But lately concentration came hard.

More young women had been arriving today than ever before, being escorted toward the harem quarters in the palace's most private sanctum. Mordecai's nerves were kept on edge as cluster after cluster of girls passed by his station, and as he surveyed them carefully, praying that his daughter not be among them.

After months of this surveillance he was still unaccustomed to it. And though to this point he had been spared the horror of Hadassah's capture, concern never ceased to possess him.

More than fear haunted him today, however. Haman, the king's vizier, was doing business in the gate, his boastful voice and ostentatious presence goading the Jew since morning.

It was not that Haman meant especially to offend Mordecai. Rarely had he ever paid much mind to the slight accountant in all the years he had served this administration. Day in and day out the grand vizier passed by the unassuming fellow who sat at the inventory bench. Day in and day out he disregarded him, interacting with the Jew only on those infrequent occasions when their business overlapped.

The only times that Haman seemed to actually have focused on Mordecai were when he had worn his fringed mantle to work, the one which designated him a member of the Jewish race. During Mordecai's early months of duty at this post he had not worn the garment. But as he had become progressively more involved with his heritage, and as he had fallen more and more in love with the teachings of Israel (scorned and avoided though they were in his youth), he had become more comfortable with those symbols which identified him with the despised ones.

It did not surprise him that Haman took note of him when he was so distinguished. Instinctively he had known the vizier would do so. So perhaps he was goading Haman subtly and quietly as much as Haman inadvertently goaded him.

Indeed, Mordecai's antipathy toward the Agagite, the Amalekite, was deep and strong. Though Haman had no idea that the old man whom his underlings had assaulted in the streets long ago was Mordecai's adopted father, he was not blind to the coolness of the Jew's greetings or the edge of bitterness which tinged their dealings.

When the accountant wore his shawl, as he did today, the Jew's antipathy was more distinct, for Mordecai himself was more distinct.

Haman did not like Jews. Though many of the race held prominent positions in Persia, the vizier looked upon them with suspicion. He did not like the way they kept to themselves, the way they attended to their own laws and customs. Strange they were, to him and to others. And sometimes he wondered how loyal they could be to the empire when they served from a divided heart.

The fact that Jews were rarely disobedient to Persian authority served only to confuse people like Haman. They were notoriously scrupulous citizens, and this in itself cast a question over them.

Be that as it may, Haman cared little what Mordecai thought of him. Jew or not, he was a fellow of small importance to the empire. As long as he did his job, Haman ignored him.

Mordecai observed the prime minister's pompous swagger as he strode here and there across the steps, giving his opinion on this matter and that, sending his valets flying on errands and commissioning his executives with various tasks. Accompanied by his closest consultants, Haman approached a broad banister which hemmed the stairs. Perched upon it was a huge stone lion, one of two which guarded either side of the entry. The Jew watched with a gimlet eye as the vizier cavalierly leaned against the royal statue. And he clenched his teeth in private disgust.

His disdainful revery was short-lived, however. Another bevy of young beauties was being brought for the king's scrutiny. As always, they were marched up the stairs, huddled and quiet. As always, they received the leering glances of a hundred onlookers. But, unlike times past, Mordecai's worst fear was realized.

He was certain he saw Hadassah. She could not be mistaken—there in the center of the little group, taller and more striking than the rest.

Anxiously she surveyed the gateway, doubtless knowing that her papa would be seated here. But before she could spy him he ducked his head, fumbling for some nonexistent object upon the floor.

Once she had been led away he rose up again, fighting back tears. Haman still reclined upon the banister, representing all that was alien. While Mordecai had publicly embraced Judaism, he felt it best for now to shield Hadassah from such a connection.

Until this calamity be past, she must not be called a Jew.

22

Hadassah walked with her dozen sister captives through the palace's echoing halls, forced along at spearpoint by a group of rigid guards. Like frightened does, the young women hung close together, fearfully eyeing their surroundings.

Soaring pillars, narrow of girth and widely spaced, lent an airiness to the enormous compound, which opened out onto vast gardens and sparkling pools. From every cornice and column top small bulls' heads stared down upon their passage, and friezes along broad staircases told tales of kings and conquerors, slaves and tribute, impressing all who traversed the grounds with the grandeur and power that belonged to rulers of this dynasty.

Crossing several colonades and entering vestibule after vestibule, the girls passed many an archway and closed door, each leading to some private sanctum of the king's courtiers and governors. Straight-backed soldiers protected every entryway, but their attire indicated that they were meant more for show than for combat. In blousy pantaloons and silken shoes, the toes upturned, they hardly looked threatening. Nonetheless, Hadassah and her companions avoided their cold gazes.

Across expansive porches the women's footsteps rang, and where they were muffled by thick Persian carpets—red and blue and gold, fringed and intricately patterned—the sound of cascading fountains, the cries of strutting peacocks, or the music of caged birds and minstrels' lyres filled the air.

It seemed a century of distance separated the queue of girls from the outside world. Ahead was a scalloped archway leading to three lobbies, each descending after the other toward a sunlit court. Soft-shoed fellows again stood bastioned alongside this portal, but by their smooth cheeks and shining chins it was clear that they were eunuchs, not warriors.

As the ladies were ushered into the first and largest of these lobbies, they were greeted by the aroma of a heavy, bulbous smoking pipe which sat upon a low table surrounded by laughing men. Propped upon embroidered pillows, they passed the pipe's hose from mouth to mouth, playing a game of dice without looking up until one of the escorts cleared his throat.

The host of the jolly party glared at the intruder.

"Another lot for the king's harem," the guide announced.

"You know where they go," the gambler sneered, flicking a hurried hand. As he surveyed the knot of girls, Hadassah took a sharp breath. She had never forgotten the angry countenance of Angus, the man who had so callously commandeered a group of harem wives the day she watched them being evicted from the palace. She had rarely thought of him during the intervening years, the memory of Vashti being the stronger image from that long-ago day. But one glimpse of his round, gloating face brought back the incident as though no time had elapsed.

Quickly the soldiers led the girls forth, through the little vestibules and toward the harem's sunstreaked court. The mocking aroma of the men's smoking pipe blended with the heady fragrance of perfumes and bath oils as the women proceeded through the last arch. Overcome with anxiety and fatigue, Hadassah doubled a fist against her stomach.

The final portico, opening on a sumptuous arboretum, framed an elegant scene. Bowers of roses and lilies, slaves with broad, feathered fans—all seemed calculated to inspire romance and a sense of luxury.

Across the pool, at the far side of the garden, the harem apartments rose in several tiers up from the court floor. They were a pretty sight at first glance, fronted by narrow catwalks and decorated with hanging plants, vines, and statuary. But on closer inspection they resembled the wall of a hive. In contrast to the open airiness of the palace compound, the quarters of the harem girls were so many claustrophobic boxes stacked atop one another.

As it dawned upon the klatch of newcomers that these were the living quarters which came with being "chosen" women, they were hushed with horror.

Hadassah wiped her palms upon her torn gown, recalling the annual village fairs she had attended with Leah's children. Just like the cattle stalls where farmers brought animals for breeding and for slaughter, so were the rooms of the harem girls.

Somewhere in the small huddle of virgins, soft weeping broke tense silence. Last night, after the girls had been led captive from several villages near Susa, they had been herded into an encampment outside the city walls. None had slept well. Certainly not Hadassah. And to face a night—endless nights—in the confines of these narrow cells was too much to contemplate.

Tears forced their way to her eyes and spilled over her flushed cheeks.

She wondered where her papa was, and why he had not been seated at the palace gate. The young Jewess sorely needed his prayers now, for he was a man of God, and he understood Jehovah's ways more than she.

23

Hadassah lay within her narrow cell, upon an even narrower cot, her head toward the back wall. It had been 24 hours since she was transported from the encampment outside Susa to this little chamber. Not once since she had arrived had any official greeted the newcomers or explained to them what was to come.

All night long she had dreamed of David, trembling into wakefulness over and over as he had turned from her in her shame. Barely could her conscious mind consider her purpose here without the most horrid fears enveloping her. Repeatedly she told herself that some salvation lay directly before her, that surely God could not mean for the king to touch her, for her life to be irrevocably sullied and her future dismissed.

Soon, she reasoned, her uncle would hear of her imprisonment. Perhaps he could bring some influence to bear . . . some plea for her release. But even as she hoped for this, her throat grew tight. She knew very well that Mordecai was no great man in the palace. Likely, the king did not even know his name.

As dawn filtered through the court's latticed ceiling, spilling past vines and laces of flowers, women up and down the hive stirred awake. Throughout the night's bleak hours, soft sobs had drifted through the thin wall of Hadassah's chamber from the adjacent room. They had quieted just before the first gray rays of morning, but now they resumed.

The neighbor was a girl of Leah's village. Close in age, Hadassah and Maryam had known each other since childhood, and the Jewess wondered how her friend would endure this misery. Maryam was a delicate child, diminutive of stature, unlike the long-legged females generally selected for the harem. Pretty as a field flower, she was painfully shy and the ordeal had already taken a murderous toll on her.

Hadassah sat up in bed and leaned around the front edge of the partition. Like a tortured convict, Maryam hunched against the wall of her room, her knees updrawn fetally, her face ravaged.

The cell to the other side of Maryam's was occupied by a Phoenician beauty. Dark and hearty, like the heathered hills of her seacoast nation, this young woman had been brought to Susa several weeks earlier. Familiarity with harem life, however, could not account for her indifferent attitude.

She sat upon the narrow walkway, her legs dangling casually between spindles of the balustrade.

Dressed in the briefest of garments, her shoulders covered only by a mass of black curls, she glanced toward the weeping newcomer with a callous sneer.

"I hope we can get some sleep tonight!" she said, loudly enough that several other girls, sporting in the pool below, responded with sly smiles.

These, like the Phoenician, evinced a careless air, and must have been her favorite companions.

"Yes—it would be nice," one replied, and the other swimmers laughed.

Hadassah bristled, creeping into the cubbyhole where her fellow villager sat.

Placing an arm about Maryam's shaking shoulders, she whispered, "Please stop crying. Everything will be all right."

"Certainly it will!" the Phoenician shrugged, poking her head into the little chamber. "Did you know that when you are at last sent before the king, you will be given your choice of dowries? Silks and jewels and precious ointments! A fortune will be yours!"

At this Maryam only wept louder, and Hadassah studied the intruder with amazement. Clearly, a passion for luxury had thus far sustained the foreigner. And perhaps such greed was what it took to endure this imprisonment.

But Hadassah had known luxury all her life. Though she was very young, she knew that such things ill served the heart.

"What of family?" she softly challenged. And then with a wistful sigh, "What of love?"

Again Maryam sobbed, and the Phoenician glanced away with a fleeting grimace. Just as quickly, however, her careless ambiance returned, and she stepped away.

"I cannot send my mother or my 12 brothers and sisters love in a bucket!" she sneered. "But they will be happy to buy food for their stomachs!"

Hadassah drew Maryam close and watched the Phoenician's determined retreat.

There were various ways to handle heartbreak, she deduced. Weeping and wailing was one, and haughtiness was another.

24

Mordecai paced the floor of his bedchamber, sleepless for the third night with thoughts of his poor Hadassah.

The house was very quiet, the servants having retired hours ago. The silence was almost oppressive as Mordecai slipped into the hall and drew near the room where his uncle, Abihail, had spent his dying days.

This room was Mordecai's study now. A large table occupied the place where Abihail's bed had been, and spread upon it were not only ledgers and accounting tables but scrolls of the Jewish Scriptures, his most prized possessions.

Softly he went to the broad desk and sat down where his servants so often found him. Since he spent more time in this place than in any other room of the house, the chambermaid knew that it was her foremost duty to keep the master's reading lamp always full of oil, his quill sharpened, and his ink bottle full.

With the passing years Mordecai had come to devote as much energy to meditating upon the Torah as to his bookkeeping. Mordecai was not an old man, but as he increasingly preferred the look of a Jew, his beard had grown patriarchally long. Streaked with silver, it gave him an appearance of age beyond his 42 years, and his shoulder-length hair lent another Hebrew touch. Yet he was still in touch with Persia, and as he walked the courts each day, he sensed more and more the disparity between the two cultures.

Tonight, restless and anxious, he tried to collect his thoughts and focus them on prayer, for he knew he was powerless to help his daughter by any human means. Yet every time he attempted to intercede for her, the image of Abihail, prone upon the bed which had sat in this very place, haunted him.

Never before had such a phenomenon interrupted his meditations. Night after night he had studied in this room, and never had the memory of his uncle interfered.

"Strange . . ." he whispered, his brow knit. "What is it?"

It was only to himself that he asked this question, but as he did, the memory of Abihail's warning, the ancient story of King Saul and Agag the Amalekite, leapt to mind.

Despite Mordecai's increased love of Israel and her traditions, Abihail's interpretation of this tale had remained gibberish to him. Suddenly, as he pondered it afresh, his skin crawled and a pervasive sense of dread enveloped him.

Rising, he stepped to the chamber window and gazed out toward the acropolis, toward the palace gate where he sat each day beneath the shadow of Haman and his cohorts.

The impression was very strong, as though imparted by the night's dark silence, that Abihail had been right. Evil stalked the royal house of Susa, evil alien to Persia as well as to Israel. Until Jehovah's will was done, it would fester, bringing misery to both cultures.

* * *

The instant dawn broke over the royal compound, Mordecai made his way through the palace gate.

All night long he had meditated upon the meaning of Abihail's warning. And though he did not yet understand just how it might involve Hadassah, concern for her well-being obsessed him.

Accountants, even of the highest stature, must have good reason to venture past the treasury rooms of Xerxes' residence. But Mordecai had a plan, one borne of the genius which darkness and solitude can generate.

"I would speak to the Keeper of the Dowries," he announced, rousing the guard from his morning post outside the harem court.

"To what purpose?" the sentry asked. "And who are you?"

"Mordecai, Chief Accountant of the Treasury. It is required that an inventory be made of the harem storehouse."

"Who requires it?" the guard challenged, wondering at the odd timing.

"I do," Mordecai simply said. "It will take several days, and we will begin straightway."

"But . . ." the guard objected, "the keeper is asleep. Can't it wait?"

Feigning impatience, the Jew looked up at the gray sunlight and sighed. "Very well. We will not waken the keeper. Only lead me to the storehouse and I will begin without him."

"But . . ."

"He may join me as soon as he likes," Mordecai snapped, rushing past the guard's objection.

Befuddled, the sentry lowered his spear and looked over his shoulder.

"I suppose it will do no harm. . . ."

"Hurry, man," Mordecai spurred him. "I haven't all day!"

Doubtfully the guard led him down the back hall of the harem. "The women are all asleep," the guard said. "See to it that you are gone before they take their morning walk. No man is to intrude upon their privacy."

"Of course," Mordecai sniffed, seeing an opportunity here. "Uh, when did you say that would be?"

"Three hours past cock crow," the guard replied. "See to it that you are nowhere near their passage."

"Certainly," Mordecai said with a bow.

They stood before the storehouse door now. Nervously the guard worked the key in the lock and let Mordecai enter the dark room. Setting a flame to the single oil lamp upon the interior wall, he stepped back and cleared his throat.

"The keeper will be informed of your presence here as soon as he wakes," he announced.

"Don't worry," Mordecai said, facing him with a condescending smile. "I am his superior. You have done well."

Bowing away, the guard softly clicked his heels together and left Mordecai to himself. The Jew beamed with private victory and began the task of counting ointment jars, his ears attuned for the sound of girlish voices in the hall.

25

Well into his "inventory" of the storeroom, Mordecai found his patience rewarded.

Girls by the dozens were emerging from their harem cells, to be herded down the hall into the morning light. They would be led to the outside garden which hemmed the palace compound, where they would enjoy one of two daily constitutionals.

Eagerly Hadassah's adopted father peered through the crack of the door, which he had purposely left ajar. He knew that the regimen of court life would repeat this spectacle again tomorrow morning. Therefore he waited to spy his daughter and to follow her beyond the wall—only to know her routine, and not, this time, to contact her. If he were successful in tracing her steps, he would venture to do so again tomorrow, and would pray for the chance to speak with her.

When at last he identified Hadassah toward the end of the line, he stifled a little cry. How sad she looked! Though she carried herself well, after the manner of her upbringing, her youthful dignity was poor compensation for the sorrow in her eyes.

Keeping close in the corridor shadows, Mordecai trailed the throng, avoiding detection by the guards who marched behind the girls.

Just as the outer garden became visible through the hallway's last door, however, Mordecai was called to a halt.

"What are *you* after?" a voice arrested him.

Wheeling about, the Jew found himself confronted by a portly lady dressed in the simple gown of a servant and bearing a tea tray.

"I . . . I . . ." he stammered.

"Yes?" the woman demanded, trying to show disapproval despite the twinkle in her eye. "You had business in the cloisters, and you saw the girls go by. It has happened here before." Then, growing very serious, she leaned near. "While your appreciation of their beauty is understandable, you must know that it is against the law to hang so close."

Waving a chubby finger under his nose, she warned, "I could turn you in, you know." With that she bustled past him. "You'd best be gone straightaway!" she called over her shoulder.

Mordecai grimaced, but something in the servant's mercy encouraged him.

"Madam," he replied, his tone anxious, "please stay a moment. I must speak with you."

Bewildered, the woman glanced back at him.

"You are very kind," he asserted, joining her near the door. "I should be forever in your debt if you might indulge me further."

The servant said nothing, but curiosity shown on her face.

"I am not what I seem," Mordecai insisted. "I am not some lecherous fool, here to spy on the maidens."

"No?" the woman said, skeptical.

"No," the Jew asserted. "I am guardian to one of those lovelies—her adopted father. You must believe me, for this hardship is very great."

The servant, knowing that such a tale could have little purpose as a lie, listened with more sympathy.

"I must know how she fares, my lady," Mordecai pleaded. "It would be worth a great deal to me."

The emphasis placed on this last statement sparked warmer interest.

"Indeed?" the woman whispered. Peering through the garden portal, she sighed, "Very well. Which child is she? And how may I serve you?"

Mordecai smiled. All morning he had counted treasure, but none of it was so valuable as this encounter.

* * *

Hadassah sat upon a bench at the nearest end of the outer court.

The helpful servant who had met Mordecai in the hall, and whose name was Dorca, assured him that the girl often sat there alone, and that he could usually find her there when the women were led to the garden.

He had waited until the second day to venture down the hall again. Now he stood within fetching distance of his daughter, trying to work up courage to call her name.

She looked thinner than he liked to see her. Surely the king's harem was afforded the finest cuisine. Was Hadassah failing to eat?

Surveying the corridor, Mordecai saw that he was alone. Leaning his head out the garden door, he saw also that there were no keepers near his daughter.

"Child!" he whispered. But his voice was lost in the sound of breeze and splashing fountain.

"Child!" he tried again.

Hadassah turned about, not certain of what she heard. And when she saw her papa, her hand flew to her mouth. Tears welled in her wide eyes, and Mordecai hushed her with a gesture.

Then, beckoning, he pleaded that she join him in the hall.

Hadassah fearfully peered about, and finding that she could do so without notice, she slipped discreetly from the bench.

Falling into her papa's arms, she quietly wept upon his shoulder.

"My Dove," he sighed, "my Myrtle Blossom. You are so thin. Are you ill, my child?"

Hadassah shook her head but continued to tremble in his embrace.

Question after question followed this as he sought to know how she was treated, how she slept, what she knew of her future.

"Tomorrow we are being sent to Hegai, Keeper of the Women," the girl informed him. "Since we arrived, we have been kept in a lesser court until he could receive us. Others have gone in already, but tomorrow my sisters and I are to go before him."

"Your sisters?" Mordecai puzzled.

"The girls with whom I entered. Hegai receives each group in its own turn."

Mordecai nodded, but grew more concerned than ever. "You must eat, my daughter. It will not go well for you here if you do not care for yourself!"

Hadassah shook her head. "But, Papa, you have taught me that certain foods are not fit for a Jew to eat. Even Leah and Moshe taught me this. There is little among the king's delicacies which is lawful."

Amazed, the Israelite studied her sincere expression. "Dear girl," he marveled, "you have always been an obedient child. But this . . ."

Words failed him. She was right, of course. Although he had not been a rigid Jew himself when Hadassah was born, he had grown more scrupulous in his observance of kosher law as she had grown. Since she had been quite little, both he and her closest kin had taught her "clean" from "unclean."

Faltering, he continued. "You are in a Persian house now. As long as Jehovah has brought you to this place, it is your duty to live according to what is provided."

He could not look at her as he said this, uncomfortable with his own logic. When she suddenly pulled away, aghast, his face burned.

"Papa!" she cried. "How can you even suggest that Jehovah has brought this trouble upon me?"

Mordecai knew all too well the reasoning which must have been hers these long days since her abduction: that surely Jehovah would not willingly subject a daughter of Israel to such humiliation, nor expect her to cooperate in any way toward its consummation.

Never had his own faith in the oracles of Mosaic law been so tested. What counsel had he for this innocent one?

A dreadful moment followed as he fought for guidance. But it was Hadassah who at last broke the silence.

"Perhaps," she softly wept, "perhaps I have done something wrong and am being punished. Perhaps I have been an evil girl, and this is my reward!" Bitterly she stared into her papa's desperate countenance. "Yes, that is it! You have told me the stories of Jehovah's vengeance—how He recompenses evil with evil!"

Flushed, she buried her face in her hands, trying to contain her tears.

Grasping at her, Mordecai clutched her to his bosom.

"You have done nothing amiss, Hadassah!" he insisted. "Even

in the moment of your capture, you honored the law."

Bewildered, the girl looked up at him. "I did?" she asked.

"Indeed!" he asserted. "Leah told me so—how you cried out in the house and in the street as you were taken."

More puzzled than ever, Hadassah shrugged. "Any girl would have done so."

"Most likely, yes," Mordecai replied. "But do you not see? This is all the law of Moses requires. When a young woman is forced into disgrace, she is absolved before God and man if she cries out. This is all that is necessary, for it is all a girl can do. Beyond this, nothing is expected . . . except that she go on living!"

Trembling, Hadassah absorbed his confident assertion. As he reached up to wipe a tear from her cheek, she clasped his hand to her lips.

"I am not wicked, then?" she whispered.

Mordecai smiled broadly and shook his head. But just as quickly he hushed her.

"I must be going," he said. "But I shall walk near the harem each day. Though I may not see you for a time, I have ways of knowing how you are. And I shall pray for you constantly. Only . . ." Here he paused, looking about warily. "One thing you must promise me."

"Yes?" she asked, picking up his careful tone.

"Have you let any of your keepers know you are a Jew?"

"I have not been asked," she said.

"Very well," he nodded. "You must keep your race a secret. Tell no one. Do you hear?"

"But, Papa, why . . ."

"It is not for shame that I say this, Daughter. It is to save your life, just as all my counsel is. Will you obey me in this?"

The girl did not understand, but complied. "I have always obeyed you, Papa," she answered.

Content now, Mordecai stepped back as though he would be going. But his daughter had fresh tears in her eyes, and reached for him pathetically.

"What is it child?" he inquired.

"David . . ." she stammered, the very word causing her to

quake. "What must he think of me now? Oh, Papa, will I ever see him again?"

Gazing upon his beloved with a heavy heart, Mordecai tried to address her gravest fear.

"Trust David to God," he said. "Trust everything to God."

ESTHER

PART IV
The Ascending Star

26

Otanes, father of Vashti, stood on the balcony once belonging to his daughter, from which she as a child had often watched the distant highway and the bustling city below.

For some months now he had known of her whereabouts, having received the information from Angus, guardian of the new harem.

Angus and Vashti had not always seen eye to eye. From the time she had been a little girl in the courts of Darius, she had resented his treatment of the king's women, and he had resented her interference, her constant suggestions and counterpoints. But the callous fellow had a soft spot for the princess in his brutish heart, and since her banishment and the reinstatement of the harem, he had turned his resentments toward Xerxes.

Otanes had been present at the banquet on the night that his son-in-law had, in besotted stupor, cast Vashti from the palace. Ever since, he had sought to know anything he could about her.

General Otanes had opted out of Xerxes' Greek campaigns, unwilling to serve Darius' successor once he had betrayed the queen. As head of one of the seven most privileged families in Persia, he had the right to bow out of military service, and he did so in spite of the fact that he had long lived and breathed to incorporate Greece into the empire.

From the night of the banquet, seething hatred of Xerxes had grown in him, festering into unrequited desire for vengeance. With the acquisition of the harem, and now talk of a new queen, he was bent fully on revenge.

Yes, he knew where Vashti was. And his skin crawled at the thought of her lonely, outcast existence in the wilds of Zagros, in the prison camp of Persia's enemies.

Since the time of Darius' forays into Europe, captured Greeks had been exiled in the stark and snowbound region east of the desert. Otanes had once seen their village, no more than a tract of wooden huts and mud houses. He had deposited a wagonload of prisoners there years before. It had been spring, and though the narrow valley was covered with cedar and mulberry trees, and wildflowers graced the rugged steeps, melting snows had left the rutted street a torrent. Sewage flowed down every path, and sickness stalked the doorways.

He could imagine his gracious Vashti, his aristocratic daughter, taunted every day, persecuted for her relation to Xerxes. He could imagine her sitting in some dark cabin, her once-royal garments long ago fallen into disrepair, and herself obliged to don the habit of strangers.

Greeks were a volatile race. He knew this, for he had observed them firsthand, both in war and as an occupying officer in their Ionian district. While they were also a merry lot, "descendants of Dionysus," god of wine, they were also captious and restive. He could imagine them dancing around his daughter, laughing and deriding as she sat unwilling beside their evening fire.

With their tight-braided hair, heavy black robes, and tattooed hands and faces, they would be leering at her. They would be swaying about her, arms raised, as pipe and drum echoed their hilarity. A thousand clacking cowrie shells, strewn upon their belts and dangling from their headdresses, would mimic their derision. And Vashti—hopeless, alien, exile of exiles—would endure the humiliation alone.

How Otanes hated Xerxes! The lad he had once loved like a son, who had grown up beside his daughter, whose alliance with her had been a coveted thing, was now the object of his fondest loathing. If he could but find a way to bring him down, to make him suffer the way Vashti surely suffered!

But he would need help. Though he was a man of influence, treachery against a king required careful planning and collusion.

Turning from the balcony, he raked his memory for faces and names of those in power who might feel antipathy toward Xerxes. It need not be antipathy of the same intensity he felt, nor for the same reasons. But if there was a seed of it anywhere, he could help it sprout and blossom.

Whether it was a good or an evil spirit which presented the suggestion to him, he knew not. Neither did he care. Indeed, it was genius which reminded him of Haman, the man currently closest to the king.

He recalled, as though it were yesterday, the little cabinet meeting held in Darius' chambers as that monarch plotted his ill-fated escapade into Greece. He recalled how Haman had disapproved the tax break given the citizens in celebration of Xerxes' upcoming marriage to Vashti.

How petty it had seemed that anyone could think a war venture required such stinginess as he proposed.

Otanes had hated Haman then. He had despised his casual disregard of Vashti and her happiness, of Prince Xerxes and his betrothed.

But now he saw Haman's resistance in a different light, in the light of his own loathing. Although Haman had risen high in the service of Xerxes, being one of his closest advisers, perhaps a shred of his former attitude remained. Perhaps Haman was not as devoted to the king as he seemed.

A smile lit Otanes' lips as he reclined upon his daughter's childhood bed. For a long time he stayed in her chamber, pondering possibilities.

27

The murals and frescoes lining the walls of the women's hall depicted a harem life unlike that which Hadassah experienced. Today, as she and her sisters were ushered away from the hive to meet Hegai, Keeper of the Women, the young Jewess wondered what artist had conceived such carefree scenes.

The pictures were from the era of Darius and his predecessors. They supposedly related to events and themes from a previous time. But Hadassah did not believe them. She did not believe that women of any harem spent most of their time laughing and dancing and sporting about. She did not believe that women who would never again see their families, women who would never have husbands of their own choice, women, who, unless the king especially delighted in them, might never twice be called by him, could be happy.

As the girls shuffled down the polished corridor, hesitantly obeying the voice of the guards, Hadassah could not imagine them ever joyous over being here. If some long-ago artist had come upon a scene of merriment and sisterly abandon, he perceived it wrongly. Perhaps he had seen girls frolicking in the pool, splashing one another and giggling, as girls will do. But he had not known their deepest hearts. Perhaps he had found them, from time to time, given to the rhythm of a pipe or tambourine. But he did not understand that they danced around heavy hearts, vainly trying to bury their misery in the moment.

If he saw the other side of their existence, he did not portray it. Such a thing would not have satisfied a king when he came to gaze upon his women. Such a thing would have cooled the ardor of a hungry monarch, passing this way to indulge his senses and select a beauty for the night.

Xerxes had not yet entered this hall, for the women were still in preparation for him. The year of his yearning for a bride was not yet over, and the selection process had not yet begun. But soon enough it would begin, as evidenced by several servants just now kneeling in the corridor with paintbrushes and putty, filling in chips, refurbishing faded colors, and updating the frescoes.

Tears threatened to spill over Hadassah's stony face as she plodded behind her sisters. She wondered if Hegai, Keeper of the Women, would interrogate her today, if he would ask her nationality or her family name. She prayed that he would not, for she did not know what she would say, and she was determined to honor Mordecai's request for secrecy.

They waited outside Hegai's door for what seemed a very long time before a portly woman came to fetch them.

Hadassah could not know that Dorca was Mordecai's "connection." But Dorca knew who Hadassah was, and she smiled especially kindly on her as she guided the virgins into the chamber.

The girls were all dressed alike, in simple cotton smocks, their street clothes having been taken from them—to be burned, they were told. Dorca understood, as they might not, that they were dressed simply and uniformly so that when Hegai looked upon them for the first time he would be able to judge them on fundamental beauty alone. No extravagant clothing, coiffure, or adornment must distract his eye from its discerning purpose.

For Hegai was seeking not just a quantity of women who would please the king, but that one special girl worthy to be queen.

Hadassah had expected Hegai to be another Angus. She was therefore very surprised when a little wisp of a man emerged from the office and came forth to greet the girls.

While Dorca introduced Hegai as the one who would manage them during their preparation, he circled the group, round and round, his hands rubbing together and his beardless chin studiously wagging this way and that.

"Uh-hmmm," he intoned, over and over, "Uh-hmmm."

Nervously, the virgins clung together as he surveyed them up and down, much as a housewife might inspect the meat hung out at market.

Yet there was much of the artist in his eye, the experienced critic. It was obvious that he knew beauty and imperfection, and could have turned away from the entwined huddle with a firm memory of each dimple, each freckle, each sweaty little hand.

Hadassah's heart pumped rapidly as he stopped near her elbow. Once more he circled the group, and then returned to her, observing her more pointedly than the others.

As he did so, his eyes brightened. And then he drew back, thoughtfully stroking his shiny chin.

"All right, all right, Dorca," he demanded in a boyish and impatient voice, "line them up."

His gaze was on Hadassah until she grew uneasy, but she followed Dorca's command and fell in line against the chamber wall, side by side with her sisters.

"Disrobe," Dorca ordered.

At this, indignant gasps arose from the little group, and the girls clung modestly to their smocks.

"It must be done," the servant insisted, trying to be callous.

Dorca had not been doing this long. She had not worked for the harem of Darius, and this routine was still uncomfortable for her. Her expression betrayed more sympathy than she liked.

As the girls shielded themselves, observing Hegai in horror, Dorca whispered, "He is a eunuch, after all. There is nothing to fear."

If the keeper heard this, he did not comment, only standing impatiently by and leafing through a sheaf of fabric samples.

When he glanced up, he again focused on Hadassah, who fumbled with her gown.

One by one the young ladies complied and cringed in shame under his scrutiny.

But it was all done quickly, and red-faced, they donned their clothes again.

Hadassah's cheeks burned and her fingers were palsied as she tugged her short tunic over her head, drew it down to her knees, and stood shaking against the wall.

"They will do," Hegai crooned.

Dorca nodded. Like so many humiliated sheep, the damsels were herded from the room until Hegai's voice stopped them.

"This one," he called to Dorca, "this one—speed her up!"

The servant followed his pointed finger and studied Hadassah with him.

Perhaps she too had seen what Hegai saw in the girl. It seemed not to surprise her when Hadassah was singled out.

"I shall," she agreed.

The young Jewess could not imagine what design they had in mind. She only crossed her arms and huddled against the back of the line.

As the virgins exited, led back to their hive, she was sure she would always feel naked. For the rest of her life.

28

Mordecai wrung his hands as he glanced between the pillars of the harem corridor. Dorca was late. Normally she met him in the hall, with word of his Hadassah, before the women's midday repast. But it was already early afternoon, and she had not come yet.

When the shuffle of her slippered feet caught his ear from behind, he wheeled about nervously.

"Madam," he greeted with a short bow, "the guard is growing suspicious. My 'inventory' work must terminate soon, and I will not be able to meet you here."

Dorca nodded. "I have expected that. But if you wish me to continue in your service, I can find a way."

The Jew smiled relief. "I do wish this," he asserted.

"Then meet me each evening in the entrance garden. I can arrange to be there after dinner," she offered.

Mordecai knew she referred to the large lobby just inside the main gate of the palace. This would be convenient to Mordecai as he sat all day upon the porch, doing his ledgers.

"Fine, fine!" he exclaimed. "The garden is open to officials of my rank. I will not attract undo notice."

Dorca's smile was reticent. "I have news today which would please most men of ambition. But in your case . . ."

"Yes," he spurred her. "It regards Hadassah?"

"She has been promoted."

Mordecai's eyes brightened reflexively. But just as fast the twinkle vanished.

"What does that mean?" he hesitated.

"Hegai sees something special in the child," the servant replied. "I just left her with the matrons where she is to enter

preparation immediately. Tradition requires a full year of puri-
fication and beautification, but your daughter's time will be
overseen with particular detail, as she is a rare find." Color fled
Mordecai's face. His middle-aged hands trembled.

"You are not proud," Dorca observed. "I feared this."

"I shall not see Hadassah after I leave this place," he sighed.
"So long as I have worked in the harem storeroom, I had the
chance to glimpse her."

The servant put forth a plump finger and stroked his sleeve.

"Perhaps the next time you see her she will be a woman in
regal splendor. My friend," she whispered, "try to see this as an
honor. Hegai is a connoisseur of beauty, and in Hadassah he has
found something rare and wonderful. The girl has been greatly
blessed."

But Mordecai only looked at the lady sadly.

"Blessed . . . or cursed?" he pondered. "I am not certain
which."

* * *

Hadassah sat upon a ledge of her private pool. Cooling fountains splashed into silent, lily-laden waters as her personal maids,
seven in all, bustled about to the commands of the head matron,
Dorca.

Here one young woman poured a flask of frankincense into
the girl's fragrant bath, and there another mixed a beautifying
paste of flour, mustard oil, turmeric, and saffron according to a
recipe recently received from India.

After Hadassah's third dip of the day into the perfumed
waters, the paste would be applied to her face and she would
sleep through one more aromatic night, still unused to the
pungent smells of her heady lair.

The evening before, a Bengalese mixture of sandalwood and
aloes had been administered, leaving her cheeks atingle, and
when it had been removed this morning, a stubborn flush had
remained part of her complexion for hours.

But all of this was supposed to perfect her—to make her more
beautiful than any other woman in the empire.

She wished that she might feel some enthusiasm for the project, which had already extended over three months. She knew that many of her harem sisters would have traded places with her at any opportunity.

The Phoenician was one of her handpicked helpers. Dorca had let Hadassah have some say in which girls were taken from the hive to assist in her personal preparation. She had selected the dark beauty from the coastland out of compassion, though the proud girl would have scorned the notion.

As for Maryam, her fellow villager, she envied Hadasssah not at all. Tender pity marked her attendance on the Jewess, for she knew Hadassah would never have chosen this "honor." She was only glad that Leah's young cousin had not forgotten her, once gone from the lower harem, and she was grateful to serve her.

Two other girls fumbled through a pile of silks and velvets, giggling and trying on today's collection of fashionable gowns, all made to complement Hadassah's natural glory to best advantage. "Oh, my lady," one exclaimed, "you will love these! Why, they are the best yet!"

Dorca, with a gesture, flicked the girls away from the rack. "The lady's linens must be changed," she barked, ordering them to the boudoir where Hadassah would recline for the night. Quickly they scurried away to change Hadassah's bedding for the second time since morning, since she had napped upon the couch, soiling it with the pastes and oils applied earlier to her skin.

Everything about this private chamber, the most indulgent in the harem, was pure luxury. Countless girls would have found life here beyond their wildest fantasies. But Hadassah had never longed for such attentions.

When Dorca set a tiny tray of stuffed prunes and iced apples before her, she only sighed. And when the matron turned away, a tear trickled down Hadassah's cheek, streaking the face cream spread upon it.

Maryam bent over her, stroking her dark curls.

"The king was seen from the harem wall today, riding with his attendants along the river," she whispered. "His royal parasol tipped back, Hadassah, and some of the girls saw his face . . ."

The Jewess did not respond.

"Oh, Hadassah, they say he is very handsome!" Maryam went on, trying to cheer her.

Still the favored one said nothing. Memories of David's golden eyes haunted her, and in her heart she walked beside him through the wheat fields.

29

Xerxes sat on the edge of his bed, staring through the twilight which crept with desert dawn through his chamber window. His huge feather pallet, elevated from the floor on golden ram's feet and enclosed with gauze draperies, cradled a young woman. Upon her face his regal gaze lingered.

He could not recall her name. He would forget her as soon as he sent her from the room. And he would never request her again.

For three months the king of the Eastern world had enjoyed the company of a new girl each evening. But he could remember only a handful. When he especially admired a certain female, he commanded her name and a brief description to be registered in his private chronicle so that he might summon her again.

Thus far the list in the royal book was quite short. And he had not bothered to request a girl a second time.

Upon dismissal from the king's chamber, each young lady was ushered to the house of the concubines, to live out her life on the chance that she might be useful in the future. Most would face years of loneliness and despair, their youthful beauty fading, their isolation prison-like despite its luxuries.

Most girls, however inexperienced, could tell after their first night whether or not they had pleased their "husband." For Xerxes was developing a volatile temper, and some of the women were thrust from the chamber before the moon had fully risen, their virginity still intact.

The sweet and simple child who now lay sleeping beside him would not encounter that side of the king. It ebbed and flowed unpredictably, and she had come to him when he was in a conciliatory mood. Nor did most of those who were rebuffed know what they had done to incur his wrath, being often among the loveliest and most charming of the "brides."

Beyond the bedroom door two guards stood, waiting on the emperor's emergence, waiting to escort the girl to the Keeper of the Concubines, the Shaashgaz, who was in charge of the second harem.

The guards had come by their work ironically. Having once served as Vashti's sentinels at the door of her private chamber, they were promoted to serve the king when she was sent away.

Their new station did not please them. They had loved the queen a long while, being her attendants when she was a child and having served her in Otanes' house. Sorely did they resent the lady's banishment, and it distressed them each time a new "bride" arrived to consort with the king.

When the door to Xerxes' chamber was at last drawn open, and the most recent "wife" stepped shakily into the corridor, they bowed rigidly toward the room's dark shadows.

They could not see the king, nor did he speak to them. Without a word he had dismissed the lady, and she stood now with the sentinels, wondering what was to come.

"You take her back," Teresh said, nodding to his companion. "I tire of this."

Bigthan, the other guard, sighed sympathetically, turning toward the errand with stooped shoulders.

Their brief interchange did not go unobserved. Otanes, father of Vashti, was rarely so near the king's chambers, especially this early in the morning. But family business had brought him at dawn to this sector of the palace, and as he passed by the emperor's quarters, he overheard the unhappy murmur.

Eager as he was for names to add to his ledger of malcontents, he registered their identity in his mental file.

These two fellows might be advantageous to him—a snare to the king.

30

Mordecai paced through the porch before the palace's garden gate, darting glances through the portal.

"Late again!" he muttered, wondering what could be detaining his contact, Dorca, this time.

The sky above the open porch was dark with thunderclouds. It was "mud month" again, a full year since Hadassah had been abducted to the harem. Anxiety had been growing in the girl's adopted father as the anniversary of her imprisonment drew near. Daily he raised earnest petitions to Jehovah, pleading for the child's release, for some miracle of intervention which would spare her from shame.

It was dinnertime throughout the palace. Most of the executives and hired help who lived outside the king's house had gone home for the evening. Mordecai would have been among them except that he had an arrangement to meet Dorca at this time each day. So far no one had questioned his lingering after hours. But he feared that sometime his "late work" might be suspect, should anyone find him pacing the open air of the garden.

The longer Dorca took, the more fidgety Mordecai became, until he heard her quick shuffle in the entry.

"I am sorry, sir," she apologized, coming upon him with her own anxieties, "I could not break away from Hegai. He kept me late tonight, preparing our dear lady for the morrow."

Though this announcement was given without hesitation, her face showed lines of regret.

"Hadassah . . ." Mordecai whispered.

"I fear so, my friend. But you must have known it was inevitable. Tomorrow is one year to the day since she was brought here. Hegai will not delay sending her to His Majesty."

"Tomorrow evening?" he said, his voice tremulous.

Dorca only nodded, and Mordecai stared at the floor through tear-filled eyes.

Hope lay in shattered shards at his feet, faith peeled itself from his heart. For 12 months he had prayed for Hadassah's salvation, finding it incredible that Jehovah could allow an innocent child to undergo such defilement.

Perhaps, he thought, perhaps he should have taught her to rebel, to risk her young life to escape the evil design. Perhaps he had been woefully remiss in suggesting to the girl that Jehovah could have brought her here. Perhaps he should have told her that she had the right to save herself regardless of the cost.

Suddenly reality clutched at him with cutting claws. Nothing he had assumed seemed apt to prove itself. Nothing he had dreamed would come true.

Dorca stood uneasily in his presence, waiting for her pittance of payment, the daily drachma of wage received for her secret service.

When Mordecai appeared to have forgotten her, she did not press him.

She said something about meeting him another day, but he did not hear her, and after she had departed he stood for a long while, staring blankly at the swirling floor.

It was not until another set of feet shuffled into the silent garden that Mordecai glanced up from his sad preoccupation. When his gaze fell upon Haman, his blood ran cold.

Stealthily he turned from the arboretum, and with a chill across his shoulders he hurried home.

Had he remained, he might have witnessed yet another rendezvous within the twilight court. For it was Otanes who had requested Haman's presence here, and moments after the prime minister's arrival, the general joined him.

The plot they discussed was private unto themselves. But in time the simple bookkeeper, the Jew who had long suspected Haman's capacity for treachery, would be their unwitting foil.

31

Hadassah stood before a long brass mirror in her private dressing room. Her seven personal maids surrounded her, their faces smitten with awe.

After four hours of helping their mistress to dress and undress, to try on one gown after another, it seemed that the most radiant combination of raiment, accessories, and hairstyle imaginable had been struck upon. Surely the keeper, Hegai, would be pleased this time when he came to inspect their handiwork. Had he not, after all, personally selected every piece of this ensemble? His temperamental taste had driven him to rage more than once this day when he had come to approve their choices. Nothing, nothing had pleased him. But surely this time there was no improving upon the lady's appearance.

Indeed, Hadassah herself was stricken speechless as she gazed upon her likeness in the mirror. Despite her fears and the dreaded ordeal which lay ahead, she could not repress a smile of surprise and delight as her reflection stared back at her.

Hardly did it seem possible that this was she! Hadassah had never been blind to her own beauty, but the regal glory of the female in the glass was beyond any she had ever witnessed before.

A lump caught in her slender throat as she turned slowly this way and that. Raising her hand to her mouth, she held back a little cry of joy.

Her keeper had chosen the most complimentary of colors for his favorite damsel. The gown, of purest linen, had been dyed a pale lavender and was cinched to her tiny waist by a broad cummerbund of royal scarlet. The scarlet, in fact, verged on magenta, with every tuck and hem piped in deep purple.

Upon her small feet were slippers of velvet, likewise of magenta hue, encrusted with gleaming rubies, violet sapphires, and amethysts. The slightly upturned toes sported tinkling bells, so teeny that they would be heard only when she walked upon the deep carpet of the king's silent chamber.

But even as she peered down at the silver ornaments where they glinted against the velvet, her heart quivered, and she could not retract the tear which gleamed upon her cheek.

David should be the first man to see this glory. Yes, David, her love—and not a Persian despot.

With numb fingers she brushed the betraying tear from her face and tried to smile again. However, when she looked once more into the glass, the image of her beloved had transposed itself over her own, with sad and hurt-filled countenance.

None of her companions saw the phantom in the mirror, and no one seemed to notice her sorrow. Save for Maryam.

As the other women laughed and giggled about her, holding the broad train of her dress to their own cheeks and dancing, her little friend came close and placed a sympathetic hand upon her shoulder.

But Maryam had no time to speak a comforting word, for suddenly the chamber door opened and Dorca bustled in, chatting excitement to Hegai, who followed with an anxious step.

"See," she exclaimed, "see! Is it not as I told you? How can she be better? She is the beauty of the world!"

The maids, who had worked so hard to achieve the effect which Hegai would now assess, held their breath as the eunuch drew into the lamplight and beheld Hadassah.

For a long while he said nothing, his face vacant. And the girls were more nervous by the minute.

Their lady was due to go before the king this very evening. If the keeper did not appreciate this work of art . . . they feared the consequences.

Slowly he circled the Jewess, uttering not a word, until even Dorca became apprehensive.

When the keeper suddenly fell to his knees, bowing over and over before Hadassah, everyone drew back in wonder.

Except for Dorca. Her expression, while one of amazement, was mixed with relief, and she nodded her head, smiling to herself.

As for Hadassah, she observed the eunuch fearfully, pondering the meaning of his strange behavior.

"My Lady!" he cried, lifting wet eyes to the Jewess, "surely you are Vashti! Surely you are the dear queen!"

Hadassah looked about her, more terrified yet, seeking an explanation.

Instantly Dorca was at her side, bowing from the waist.

"Hegai is right, my child," she agreed. "How you resemble our banished Lady!"

Recalling the one time that she had been privileged to look upon the queen, when as a child she had peered between the spindles of the garden balcony, Hadassah turned again to the mirror and with hesitation surveyed her reflection.

A chill passed down her spine and she grasped her skirt with a trembling hand. Long ago as it had been, the recollection of Vashti matched that in the glass, and Hadassah braced herself against vertigo.

But now Hegai was standing, and as the girl studied the mirror, Dorca handed the keeper the cape which he had designed for this ensemble.

Stepping behind the Jewess, the eunuch tenderly draped the stole around her shoulders and gazed with her into the glass.

"It is a miracle!" he cried.

And it was. The purple stole, embroidered with pink and lavender irises, drew the entire outfit together, lending Hadassah an unmistakable look of royalty.

Feeling faint now, the girl put forth a hand, and Hegai held her upright.

"It is fitting that you should have a new name," the eunuch pronounced. "A new name for a new life. You shall be called 'Esther,' for you are worthy of nothing less."

Hadassah clutched his hand more firmly, her breath coming anxiously. Esther? No more dreadful designation could be applied to a Jewess, for Esther, or Ishtar, was the most pagan of goddesses, the Astarte of the Canaanites, the Aphrodite and the

Venus of the Greeks. Goddess of fertility and sexuality, she was a demeaning label for any girl who loved Jehovah.

Shaking her head, Hadassah wished to cry aloud. But, remembering Mordecai's injunction to keep her race a secret, she choked back her horror.

And now Hegai was standing before her, placing a fresh orchid in her raven hair and weaving its short stem between the intricate waves.

Bidding her take his arm, he turned her about and led her forth from the chamber.

She would not remember the long walk down the palace's cold corridor. She would not notice the awe-filled faces of all who saw her, nor would she hear the gasps of wonder which followed her bleak passage.

She walked into a void, mystified that faith should have failed her.

32

Esther stood within the king's dimly lit chamber, the door having been closed behind her.

Xerxes, Emperor of the East, master of the greatest empire on earth, had not yet acknowledged her presence, but only sat brooding at his northern window. He had no reason to pay this new "bride" any more mind than he had paid the dozens brought before.

It was true that Hegai had personally escorted Esther to his door rather than sending her with a guard. It was true that the eunuch had, upon introducing her to the bridal suite, emphasized her new name. And if anything should have piqued the king's interest, it would have been this.

For though the emperor was a devout adherent of the one god Ahura-Mazda, the name "Ishtar" in any language had a way of thrilling the blood of most men.

It had troubled the keeper when Xerxes had ignored the introduction, receiving Esther with a flick of the hand and failing to even turn his head toward her. But Hegai had shut the door upon the couple, confident that when the king did glimpse the girl he would succumb to her humble charms.

And humble she was. This too might have troubled Hegai. He might have wondered just how adept the young virgin could be at seduction. But he passed off the concern. What need had such beauty of experience or of effort? The fact that any female so designed was flesh and blood, and not a statue conceived by wild fantasy, would be enough to secure her place in Xerxes' favor.

For no man could fail to love her. No man could ignore her, Hegai was certain. Even he, stripped of his masculinity, rendered impotent from birth that he might serve the palace with docile single-mindedness—even he was moved in his own way by this girl.

So Esther stood, unspeaking in the shadows, awaiting whatever lay ahead.

Never had she prayed so fervently as during these moments. If Jehovah intended to intervene, He must do so now. For weeks she had, in hours of fear, rehearsed the childhood lessons of Judaism learned upon Mordecai's lap, memorized at Leah's knee. Tonight, however, they eluded her, and she found herself cast helplessly upon blind trust.

Somehow, though it made no sense to her, she must accept whatever should happen here. Having done all she could to please Jehovah, she must abandon herself to any tyranny that God might permit.

With an empty sigh she looked down at the garment that Hegai had prepared for her. Each girl was allowed to choose the outfit she would wear upon her "wedding" night, heeding or disregarding Hegai's advice as she wished. But Esther had not quibbled, having determined ahead of time that she would accept the eunuch's advice. Truly his taste was impeccable, and he had done well by her.

The garment symbolized the end of life as she had known it. It was, in fact, all she had in this world. Every young woman, upon the day she went before the king, was allowed to take from the harem whatever she wished. Most girls had given this privilege much advance thought, gathering up enough jewels, gold, spices, and fine fabrics to secure their futures and the futures of their loved ones beyond the palace walls for years to come. But Esther had requested nothing but the clothes upon her slender frame.

This was all she needed. Material goods would never cheer a future without family . . . without David. . . .

It seemed she waited in the shadows for an eternity, though by the wintry glow of sunset beyond the king's window it had been only moments since she arrived.

Quivering, Esther surveyed her intended. Though he was in silhouette against the ruddy night, she could see that he was a tall man, and strong. His features, framed by the departing light, were regal; his hair, where it spilled in waves to his shoulders, was lustrous and dark.

Still, until she could see his eyes, she would know little about him save what rumor had imputed to him. And rumor had painted a fearful picture—one of capriciousness and cruelty.

Through the window's scalloped arch the famed Zagros mountains loomed, distant and austere.

Was the emperor at prayer? Esther wondered. The faraway mountains were sacred to the Persians, she knew, especially to those who followed the teachings of Zoroaster.

But, then, she reminded herself, Xerxes was the man who had sent his queen into exile. Could such a creature bear a bone of religious devotion in his body? Ahura-Mazda, she had heard, was very much like Jehovah—God of the universe, a kind and just deity. If it were possible that the Persians received some spiritual light from their worship, Xerxes had surely turned from it.

It must have been the descending dark which spurred the king to turn at last from the window. When he did, he did not immediately focus on the girl in the shadows. It seemed, in fact, that he had forgotten her very presence. And Esther was surprised to note that his eyes, now visible in the lamplight, bore a heavy sadness. Far from indicating a cold heart, they betrayed a wounded spirit, taking Hadassah aback.

"Well, let us see what we have here," the emperor suddenly commanded, gesturing her forward, though still not looking upon her.

Cautiously the virgin Jewess stepped into the lamp's exposing glow, and at last the king glanced up from whatever wistful thoughts had held him.

As he did, his expression grew from one of apathy to one of incredulity. Gripping the bedpost, he held himself steady and slowly sank to the mattress, sitting palefaced as one who witnessed an apparition.

"Lord Ahura-Mazda," he gasped, "can it be? Vashti, my bride!"

Esther, rigid with fright, dared not contradict the king.

Finding strength to rise, Xerxes approached her, his lips trembling.

"Thank you, Ahura," he was whispering over and over. "Thank you."

Reaching for Esther, he enfolded her in strong arms, repeating Vashti's name in her ear.

Terrified, the girl struggled in his embrace. But he allowed no resistance.

"My child," he groaned, "bless me. Do not deny your king . . . your husband. Let me believe in miracles."

Pressing his lips to her neck, he drew her cape from off her shoulders, stroking her bare arms with gentle hands.

Dizzy from his persistent caress, Esther closed her eyes, and the lamplight yielded to the night.

* * *

Somewhere deep in the Zagros, Vashti, deposed Queen of the East, lurched upright on her bed of animal skins.

Her face, still lovely despite the lines which loneliness and alienation had traced, peeked through the darkness toward her distant royal city.

Something had roused her from near slumber— some dread awareness.

She was alone in her wooden hut. Everyone else in the village was asleep. But there would have been no consolation even in brightest daylight. Had she spoken fluent Greek, none of her fellow exiles would have cared for her plight.

Lying down again, she listened to the beating of her solitary heart. Somehow she knew that Xerxes was not alone. Somehow she sensed the rising of another star.

ESTHER

PART V
For Such a Time as This

33

The sky over Susa was a rainbow of color. Phosphorescent greens, blues, and vermillion lit up the night in explosive auroras.

Xerxes had spared no expense in celebrating his marriage to Esther. Within a week of her coming to him a holiday had been declared, imperial gifts in the form of reduced taxes had been given the provinces, and people had exchanged lavish presents.

The wedding itself, held in Persepolis, was unparalleled in Persian history. And immediately following, the king announced a banquet in Susa's royal house. "Esther's banquet," he called it, a reception second in grandeur only to the many-month celebration at which he had banished Vashti.

Fireworks had been displayed each evening for a week, igniting the sky above the acropolis with symbolic splendor, because the emperor, after years of disappointment, misery, and futile endeavors to find happiness, was experiencing life once again.

Daily he called his new queen to dine with him in his private suite, and nightly he loved her with an ardor unknown since last he had lain with Vashti.

He assumed that Esther must be as happy as he was, though not once had he asked her. In fact, he knew nothing of Esther's heart, reading in her only what he wanted to read. And what he wanted to read was that she was the answer to prayer, the closest thing to Vashti returned to him.

There was another man, however, who wondered how Esther felt. She had never been out of his thoughts since the night she was abducted to the palace.

David stood at his village's western gate, watching the bursting aura across the desert.

Hope had died when Hadassah was taken to the king's chamber.

David had known what evening that was. He had counted the dawns and sunsets leading to it, 365 of them.

As he stood tonight at the low village wall, studying the celebrating flashes, each explosion sent a spear through his heart. He was no warrior. He had no weapon with which to fight back—only the farmer's hoe upon which he leaned. And the acropolis, bathed in azure and scarlet, mocked his poverty.

Should he wonder any longer how Hadassah felt? Was she not the owner of an emperor's embraces, pride of a sovereign's heart, wealthiest woman on earth?

David gripped the handle of his hoe in a stranglehold. Perhaps he should wrap the long tool in fancy paper and send it to the palace, he thought cynically. It was all he could offer as a wedding gift. It was all he possessed.

Glancing heavenward again, he shrugged and dropped the hoe against the wall. Downcast, he plodded home, pushing against the weight of a hollow heart.

34

Clouds of nearing spring swept over Susa's acropolis. Queen Esther, hastening through the inner court, glanced skyward but did not see the cottony tufts, her mind speeding higher, seeking Jehovah in earnest prayer.

She would be with her papa in a few moments. Using her regal position to advantage, she had arranged to "interview" the bookkeeper for a position as her private accountant.

She had let no one know of her relationship to the Jew, in accordance with Mordecai's wishes. It was only under the guise of business that she could even properly be seen by any male other than her husband. But she had made certain that no one else would be present, sending all her maids off on errands and scheduling the "audience" in an unguarded alcove.

"Let nothing hinder this stolen moment," she pleaded as she hurried toward the rendezvous.

Passing through the final vestibule before the garden, she came to a frozen halt, a deep shadow having fallen across her path.

High above, upon a fluted pedestal, the enormous black stone head of a sacred bull stared down upon her. Fully as great in length as the lady's own height, and half as wide, it hovered over her like a disapproving giant. And across the broad aisle was its partner, equally brooding.

Though she was queen, she had not been trained for the part. She was still a humble Jewess, quiet daughter of a quiet man.

The bulls threatened her, doubting her ability, suspecting her.

For a long moment she hesitated beneath their austere gazes. Gleaming in the brilliant sun, they leveled dark questions at her, their cold, polished eyes and heavy brows deflecting all signs of weakness.

Quietly she eased past them, entering the garden and the alcove through a haze of self-castigation.

But when she saw Mordecai, her countenance brightened. "Papa!" she cried, flinging her arms wide and flying to him. Mordecai drew back, shaking his head and bowing.

"My Queen," he hailed.

Horrified, Esther stared at him, hot tears rising to blind her. "Papa?" she returned. "It is I, your Hadassah."

But Mordecai could only gaze speechlessly upon her.

Did he disapprove as well, she wondered? Did he recoil from the stain upon her life?

In agonized silence the girl turned her face to the floor, and Mordecai, seeing her distress, at last found words.

"Hadassah . . ." he whispered. "It is only that you . . . you are royalty now. And a woman, a beautiful woman . . . not a girl. Hardly would I recognize you, did I not know you so well."

Though this acknowledgment bore a sting, a smile parted Esther's lips, and with a sigh she reached for him again.

"It has been so long . . ." Mordecai cried, returning the embrace. "Can you still care for this old man—this . . . commoner?"

"Papa!" Esther rebuked him. "Do not speak so!"

But it was Mordecai's turn to smile. And clinging, they wept together.

Just as quickly, however, the Jew held her at arm's length, his face etched with urgency.

"Child," he whispered, "bear with a bit of whimsy, if you will. There is something I must tell you."

Esther studied him quizzically, wondering at the anxious mystery in his tone.

"Of course, Papa," she nodded. "What troubles you?"

Casting a wary glance over his shoulder, he continued, "There is evil afoot in this place. I have felt it for months, and today, on my way here, I witnessed it firsthand." Then, bowing again, he seemed to beg her indulgence, and she spurred him.

"Papa, I am your Hadassah," she asserted. "Please go on."

"Perhaps it was my imagination . . ." he hesitated. "But as

I came down the main corridor, I passed by two men who consulted together, dressed like guards—royal guards. Both were tall, and very strong, as though . . ."

"The king's doorkeepers," Esther guessed. "Dark and bearded?"

"Yes, yes!" Mordecai enthused. "You know them, then?"

Esther's mind flashed to the night she had first been introduced to the king's chamber, and she nodded with wistful sadness.

"Then I am not mistaken!" the Jew determined. "The king is in danger!"

Quickly reciting the conversation overheard in the hall, he warned the queen that this very evening Xerxes' life was at stake. "'When he is asleep, after the chamberlain puts out his light . . .'" he quoted them. Then, rubbing his hands nervously together, Mordecai continued, "Oh, child, they thought they were alone, and when I suddenly rounded the corner, coming upon them, they covered their plot with idle chatter."

Esther's face grew pale, and drawing close, she confirmed Mordecai's fears. "There are many who hate the emperor," she agreed. "Many loved Vashti, and I have sensed jealousy for that lady in the air since the day I took the throne. . . ."

"Then, my child," Mordecai cringed, "you also could be in danger!"

Esther shivered, and placed a cold hand on her papa's arm.

"You shall be rewarded," she commanded him. "I do not know the king well, but I know he honors his friends."

Mordecai glanced at the tiled floor, an ironic smirk working at his lips. "I, a *friend* of Xerxes," he laughed. "I dare say, I love him less than anyone could."

Gazing into Hadassah's sympathetic eyes, he shook his head. "There is more . . . much more than I have told you," he insisted. "There is more evil here than a plot between bedroom guards."

The queen awaited an explanation, but he could give none. It was an intuition of the blood which told him—an insight of the spirit giving warning.

"In time we shall see it all," he said. "For now I know nothing."

Esther felt the pallor of his prophecy, and did not question it. Recalling the dark gazes of the garden bulls, the black gleam of their marbled eyes, she knew he spoke the truth.

The palace of Persia was a battlefield, and the opponents played a contest more profound than politics.

35

The incident with the king's guards was to be only the first skirmish in the supernatural battle staged in Persia's royal house. Of all the people in the land, only Mordecai the Jew saw it as something more than a human battle. And even he could not foresee the part it played in the greater drama.

Otanes and Haman certainly did not perceive the working out of a higher plan. To Otanes, the attempt to overthrow Xerxes was a justified act of retaliation. To Haman, whose assistance Otanes had promised to reward, the goal had been personal advancement.

When the general and the prime minister lost the first round, they determined even more sincerely to work for Xerxes' demise.

In the executive courtyard they met this afternoon, beneath the swaying shadows of two corpses, the bodies of Bigthan and Teresh, suspended from the gallows of Xerxes' wrath.

"Who revealed the plot?" Otanes snarled, disappointment heavy beneath his breath.

"A minor executive," Haman replied, "the Jew who now keeps the books for Queen Esther."

His loathing of the race readily surfaced, and Otanes shrugged. "The one who used to sit at the gate? Head of inventory?"

"The same," Haman smirked. "One can never be too careful."

"Careful?" Otanes sneered. "The fools must have heralded their plan upon the palace roof!"

"Well, it is done now," Haman sighed, glancing up at the dead men on the gallows.

Otanes said nothing, deep in thought. Then, having struck upon a new idea, he eagerly pursued a different tack.

"Haman, how would you like your reward *now* . . . before the deed is done?"

The prime minister studied the general, incredulous. Leaning forward eagerly, he dreamed of glory.

* * *

Trumpets blared in the gate of Susa's palace. Haman was entering, and everyone prepared to do him homage.

Xerxes, prey to the blindness common to the powerful which renders them insensible to dangers directly beneath their noses, saw Haman as a loyal adviser, a man of duty and accomplishment who had served his father well and who served his own administration admirably. When Otanes came before the king praising the prime minister and suggesting that some great honor be heaped upon him, Xerxes, wishing to appear magnanimous, elevated the Agagite, establishing his position as second in command of the empire. With this, he went so far as to require all servants and princes of the royal house to bow down whenever the man passed by. Refusal to do so would not only merit Haman's disapproval but would invoke the wrath of the emperor himself.

In reality, the "advancement" carried little political clout. Haman was already grand vizier. But this public commendation on the part of Xerxes raised his prominence in the eyes of all, forcing them to render obeisance, however begrudgingly.

Haman was not a popular figure. He had few admirers and fewer lovers. But since the king's edict had been enacted, it could be suicide to ignore him.

Therefore, it was with incredulous wonder that the palace servants, bowing as Haman entered the gate, observed Mordecai's rebellion.

The Jew would not bow. The Jew would not pay homage to an Agagite.

Stiff and austere, the gray-bearded Hebrew sat behind his accounting bench upon the public porch, unyielding as the prime minister passed his way.

Until Mordecai foiled the assassination attempt, Haman had brushed elbows with the Jew on numerous occasions but had paid him little mind. He was, as he had told Otanes, a "minor executive," and a Jew at that.

But this day, when Mordecai drew attention to himself through blatant disrespect, Haman had more reason than ever to notice him. In an instant the Jew leapt from obscurity to public prominence.

Haman, stopping directly before the bookkeeper's table, said nothing, waiting for his compliance. But Mordecai's behavior was not the product of oversight. Directly he stared back at the prime minister, refusing to bow, until Haman's face flushed crimson with anger, and amazed whispers fluttered about the court.

Had Haman only rebuked him, the Jew's position might not have seemed so precarious. But when the Agagite turned for the palace door, entering the royal house without a word, retribution was all the more imminent.

Once Haman was out of sight, the spectators gathered around the quiet Hebrew like astonished gossips.

"Why are you transgressing the king's command?" they queried.

Mordecai, a very private man, had never drawn so much notice. But an answer was ready on his tongue.

Stroking his frosted beard, he framed the reply with dignity.

"Because," he said, "I am a Jew."

36

Haman paced the king's council chamber, counting the alabaster tiles with his toes, his face etched with feigned frustration.

"How your royal patience must have been strained all these years, Your Majesty! I do not know how you have endured it," he exclaimed.

Xerxes leaned forward upon his throne, his own expression one of bewildered scrutiny.

"Say again, Haman," he implored. "These folk to whom you refer—they have been party to sedition?"

"Indeed, Your Highness. But you must know it. Surely—oh, I see . . . How clever of you to test me, Sire. You wish a fuller disclosure of their activities?"

Xerxes, not wishing to appear unaware of the supposed dissension within his kingdom, only nodded.

Haman, with a sigh of deep concern, ceased his pacing and rubbed his hands together. "O King, live forever!" he intoned. "You know that there is a certain people . . ." And here he peered about him, as though concealing their identity was of critical importance to the safety of the realm, ". . . a certain people scattered abroad and dispersed among the folk of all the provinces of your kingdom. And their customs are different from everyone else's. Nor do they keep the king's laws," he lied. Then, with a quick and deliberate pronouncement, he concluded, "Therefore it is not for the king's profit to allow them to continue!"

The emperor sat back, studying Haman blankly. Dare he let on that he was less informed than his key adviser regarding such widespread subversion? And dare he question the very man whose reputation he had so recently secured, whom he had just publicly endorsed as second-in-command of his entire empire?

He knew not of whom Haman spoke. He did not know that this tax pirate had a personal vendetta against a single Jew, a modest bookkeeper. He did not know that Haman's wounded pride could prompt him to appeal for a pogrom against an entire race.

Xerxes had his own struggle with pride. Therefore, rather than admit to ignorance, he would affirm Haman's stand.

Swallowing hard, he considered the prime minister's intentions.

"What do you wish of me?" he asked at last.

A gleam flashed through Haman's eyes. "If it please the king," he said with a low bow, "let it be written that these people may be destroyed."

He hesitated to look upon Xerxes. Quickly he added, "I will pay 10,000 talents of silver to the mercenaries who carry out the business . . . for the king's treasuries, of course."

Haman, still in a bowed posture, remained that way for some seconds as the king surveyed him with a drumming heart. When Xerxes finally spoke, a thrill of certain vengeance shot through the Agagite.

Taking his royal ring from off his finger, the one with which he sealed all documents of law, the emperor handed it to Haman.

As the prime minister held forth a sweaty hand to receive it, Xerxes grasped at a show of power. "Keep the silver," he flaunted. "Go and do as seems good to you."

37

Xerxes ambled through the court of his harem, luxuriating in the fleshly beauty of half-clad women who, on cue, sported before him in their garden pool.

Never let it be implied by blushing cheek or hesitant gyration that any girl upon whom he gazed was obliged to tease him. The flirtatious cavorting must always be spirited, as though prompted by ardent love.

After all, were not his visits to this sanctum very rare? Especially since he had taken Esther to wife, he had seen little reason to grace this court with his regal presence.

As compared with previous Persian monarchs, Xerxes' attention to his concubines was becoming more and more casual. In fact, now that he had married the lovely Jewess, his lifestyle bordered on monogamy.

It was true that he still allowed his underlings to continue bringing beautiful young virgins to his palace, and that he had at his disposal an entirely new bevy of maidens ready for initiation into the house of wives. But he had virtually ignored them.

As he passed through the garden this evening, it was with only cursory interest that he lingered over them. He was headed for Esther's suite.

Usually he met with his bride in his own chamber. But he had tired of that, and now wished for new surroundings. What he did not anticipate was that meeting Esther upon her own ground would reveal a side to her that he had not yet seen.

Indeed, there was much about his wife which was unknown to him. For months now he had freely called her "Vashti," reveling in her embrace as though it were the embrace of his first love. Many times Esther would have addressed this fact; she would

150

have challenged her "husband" regarding his illusions. But she had never found the strength, had never felt it her place to do so.

Tonight, as she waited in her room, in lonely anticipation of the king's arrival, some seed of self-assertion awoke within her. Perhaps it had cracked open days before, sending forth a shoot of courage when her papa had spoken of the evil in this place. But tonight it struggled for expression, and as she heeded its demands, she steeled herself against Xerxes' touch.

When he appeared in her doorway, however, he was his commanding self, the sovereign who had forced her obedience months before. His striking frame nearly filled the entry, his handsome bronze face irresistibly appealing.

Had his eyes not beseeched her, she could have been angry with him. But in his face she read his humanity—the vulnerability which allowed him to be wounded as much as he had wounded others.

As he approached across the room with admiration in his gaze, she could almost believe that he loved her—*herself*, Esther . . . Hadassah.

If, as it seemed, she was destined to remain forever with him, she must believe this. Life would be unending torment otherwise. And though she did not love him, she might be persuaded to try . . . if only . . .

But when Xerxes spoke, she knew again the truth.

"My Lady," he said, sighing a smile, "you are, of all women, worthy of this chamber. Only such great beauty as yours should enter here."

Esther had not risen from her seat beside the fireplace. Sadly she studied the shadows between the flames, the amber light betraying her heavy spirit.

"Sir," she whispered, "you often say such things, thinking they do me honor. And so they do. But they also prick my heart."

Xerxes had never heard her speak so. In fact, in all these months of marriage her heart had remained a closed scroll, nor had he attempted to read it.

Stepping close, he leaned over her, passing a gentle finger across her cheek.

"You are not yourself tonight, my dear," he crooned.

Esther pulled away and surveyed him quizzically.

"I suppose that depends upon who you think I am. If you refer to me, Esther, I am indeed myself," she asserted. "If you think of me as Vashti . . . I am not."

There. It had been said. Xerxes was incredulous—not at the revelation, for he knew he clung to illusion. But at the girl's newfound courage he was taken aback.

Still, Esther took a deep breath and added, "Is it not true, My Lord, that you did not admire *me* when you entered the room, but your memory of Vashti as she once graced this chamber? And is it not true that you still love her, and have never loved me?"

Xerxes did not readily answer. Lowering his eyes, he shunned her observation.

"By the faith of Ahura-Mazda," he swore, "I have loved you!"

At this Esther stood and faced him squarely.

"You claim the blessing of your god upon our union?" she challenged. "Do you not call him God of the Universe, King of Heaven?"

The emperor could have been offended by her tone, but instead he nodded solemn agreement.

"Then," the young Jewess declared, "he never countenanced the treachery which sent your first queen from you, and which brought me to your bed. He did, perhaps, allow all this for some cause unknown to us. But he did not ordain it. And he will not suffer the lie forever."

Esther's pulse quickened with the confrontation, and for a long moment Xerxes stood confounded by her discernment.

Longing to draw her to him, he at last turned for the door, leaving the room with stooped shoulders and wondering if he should ever hold her again.

38

The rackety clatter of large bone dice was muffled by the thick Persian carpet in Haman's council chamber.

Three young men, longtime servants of the prime minister, were huddled about a circle of goat hide upon which were mystical designs and a chart of the houses of the heavens. Over and over they rolled three "purim," the bone counters, against the leather map. As the pieces took their places upon the star chart, the men chanted out the weeks and months of the year.

For the chart was not only an astrological map but a calendar, and the bone dice chose not only certain celestial positions but their corresponding dates as well.

Night after night, the men had met to carry out the strange ceremony, and night after night Haman had watched them, pacing anxiously along the carpet and asking the interpretation of their findings.

He had chosen these fellows to perform this rite because they had always served him well. Having been his students years before in the accounting school, they had risen with him in imperial administration.

The sacred "purim," obtained by Haman from the palace priests, were used to determine the times and seasons of special events. Such dice had been rolled when Xerxes and Vashti awaited the pronouncement of their wedding date, and they were being rolled now to set the date of the pogrom against the Jews. Normally only the priests would have handled the "purim." But the case to be decided here was a matter of national security, Haman claimed, and government officials could be ordained to determine the times for such things.

As the servants tossed the counters again and again, brows

dotted with sweat from the hours-long ordeal and throats rasping from interminable chanting, they rocked to and fro upon their heels, their knees sore with chafing against the woolly carpet.

At last, however, one of the men gave a cry.

"We have a match!" he declared.

"A match?" Haman repeated, hesitant to enjoy the possibility.

"It is definite, Master!" another confirmed. "The number of our throw corresponds perfectly with the number on the dice, and it has fallen upon the same number upon the calendar."

"Yes . . . yes . . . what is it?" Haman demanded, weaving his fingers together.

"The twelfth month, the month of Adar," the servant replied.

Haman was delighted to have an answer, but somewhat put off by the fact that Adar was yet 11 months away. Nevertheless he asserted, "Very well. And now, what of the day?"

"By tradition, sir," the third reminded him, "the day is always one number larger than the month. We need not throw the purim to decide this."

Haman's eyes brightened. Of course he remembered this.

"Then," he reckoned, "the annihilation of the king's enemies is set for the thirteenth of Adar."

"Indeed," replied the first. "Now, sir, may we know against which people we have been performing this duty? Who exactly are these enemies of the king?"

Haman was not a very superstitious man, but he would not risk the goodwill of the purim by prejudicing his servants in the performance of their task. Therefore he had not told them just whose lives were at stake in the coming purge. Now that the date had been established, however, he could let them in on the secret.

Drawing them to him in a tight circle, he whispered, "Do you recall, years ago, how I spared you from judgment in the matter of an old man's death—an old fellow you challenged in the streets one New Year's Eve?"

Thinking back, the men did recall an incident in which they had in youthful frolic done bodily injury to an elderly gentleman. Unfortunately, the old man had been too frail to survive their exuberance, and had died shortly thereafter.

"We recall, Master," they acknowledged.

"Well, he was not the last of his race to receive a kick from you."

Haman's toothy grin sent chills down the servants' spines. Though they admired their master, something about him could chill the coldest heart.

"He was a Jew, was he not?" one asked.

"You have a keen memory, Drusal," Haman commended him. "A sneaking, money-grubbing Jew. The kingdom will be better off without his kind."

Drusal and his companions surveyed one another silently. Through each of their minds flashed the image of Abihail, the innocent one whom they had shamefully attacked.

He had not seemed a wealthy man. Had he not been dressed in a farmer's rags?

And he had not appeared bent on any treachery that long-ago night as he carried his wriggling bundle through the dark street.

But they would not correct Haman on these points. Their duty had been done. It was now left to them to deal with their consciences, to find ways to sleep each night for the next eleven months.

39

Mordecai the Jew sat in the public square outside the palace of Susa, sifting ashes through his fingers and pouring them over his head. The ashes mingled with the silver streaks of his already-gray beard and clung to his eyebrows. Ashes covered his shoulders and the pathetic garment of sackcloth which he had donned.

Upon the ground he sat, rocking to and fro, as all about him Jewish brothers and sisters from all parts of Susa—from the fine mansions lining the Shapur River to the filthy ghettos on the far side of town—chanted the horrid tale of Haman's hate.

This very day the edict, sealed with the king's own signet ring and declaring the destruction of their entire race, had been delivered by courier throughout the capital. Even now copies were being sent to every province of the empire, declaring the date for the annihilation of the Jews.

Confusion reigned, among Gentiles as well as Hebrews. For this pronouncement had not been preceded by any warning, and there had not been any escalation of bias against this group of people. For decades, Jew and Gentile had coexisted peacefully, with only occasional spates of racial tension coloring their interaction.

Certainly everyone knew that the Jews were an odd lot. They themselves were fond of acknowledging that they were a "peculiar people," having their own brand of history, their own slant on imperial politics, and even their own code of religious laws and traditions. However, they were known to be quiet folk, generally honest and reputable citizens of the kingdom. Few could think of any reason for this sudden turn of policy on the part of the emperor.

But Mordecai knew the reason, and there were others who suspected that it was due to his refusal to bow to the prime minister that Haman had set the king's heart against the Hebrews. Even those who suspected this, however, were amazed that Xerxes could so lightly be moved against such a large portion of the population.

Had they known that Xerxes had signed the edict without even inquiring as to the identity of the targeted group, they would have been even more chagrined at their sovereign's shallow nature.

Tapping into palace rumor, Mordecai had learned more than most about the details of the case. In fact, because he was so personally involved, friends brought him every word they heard from the interior. And so he knew even the amount of money that Haman had volunteered to pay for the extermination.

It had been noon when the edict was posted in Susa's square. By early evening, thousands of horrified Jews and their sympathizers had crowded into the square outside the palace.

No one was allowed inside the King's Gate while dressed in mourning, but the cries of protest and pleading which filled the dusky air had surely reached the ears of Xerxes, who, it was reported, sat at wine with Haman himself.

Of course, word of Mordecai's likely involvement in all that had come to pass had spread throughout the Jewish community. He could have been the most despised man among his brethren. But instead, his refusal to accommodate the pride of unpopular Haman had become a symbol of racial integrity, and Mordecai had in a few short hours been catapulted to the prominence of an ethnic hero.

As for Mordecai, there certainly had been moments since news of the edict when he had regretted his rebellion, wondering if Jehovah had been with him. It was true that the proposed move against the Jews was still nearly a year away, but no amount of time would save his people. Were they to gather together in force even now, they could not succeed against the entire empire of Persia.

However, in the presence of this reassuring company Mordecai found his faith uplifted, and felt hope in the midst of hopelessness.

As he sat, eyes closed and head tilted back, imploring heaven, he felt a tap on his shoulder. Peering above, he found a grandly attired fellow bending over him.

By his appearance he was a eunuch, bald and clean of face, decked in pure linen embroidered with gold. In strange attitude he bowed to the Jew, holding forth a bundle of even finer clothing in his arms.

"Mordecai?" he greeted.

"I am."

"Our Lady, the Queen, has sent me to you, pleading that you take these garments and cease your mourning."

Mordecai stared at him in mute consternation.

"You are Mordecai, the bookkeeper to the Queen, are you not?" the servant repeated.

"I am," he replied again.

The eunuch, maintaining his dignity despite uneasiness at the task he had been given, went on.

"Our Lady's maids brought her word of your condition, saying you were in this square. The queen begs you to take off your sackcloth and accept her gift."

Straightening his back, Mordecai insisted, "Does the queen not understand the reason for my grief? Has no one told her?"

The servant, unused to questioning a royal command, could only shrug. And Mordecai, clearing his throat, answered, "Tell Our Lady that her lowly employee appreciates her concern. But . . . I cannot accept her gracious gift."

Stunned, the eunuch stepped back, looking awkwardly at his bundle.

But seeing that Mordecai was intent upon his decision, he bowed slowly once more and retreated toward the palace.

All about the bookkeeper a huzzah of astonishment rose as folk observed Mordecai's daring. His status as hero grew on the instant, his name becoming a chant which filled the sky above the court.

"Mordecai, Mordecai," it rang, the syllables exciting the twilight. As dark descended, the name continued to mark the moments until the Jew, sitting calmly in an attitude of prayer, was again roused by someone's hand.

Looking up once more, he found yet another eunuch standing above him, this one even grander than the last.

"I am Hathach," the servant announced, a hush coming over the crowd, "one of the king's eunuchs, appointed to Her Majesty."

This man's demeanor was more challenging than that of the last. Had Mordecai not learned the confidence of faith, he might have trembled before him.

"Her Majesty, Queen Esther, wishes to know the meaning of your behavior this day, and the purpose of this . . . gathering."

This last word, preceded by an aloof glance about the court, was said with a sneer.

But Mordecai cared not for Hathach's assessment. Gathering his dusty garment to his chest, he looked upon the eunuch with equal condescension.

"Can it be, sir," he inquired, "that Our Lady is not privy to the news of Persia? Does the palace so insulate her that she has not heard of the king's edict? And is it possible that such a notable as yourself can likewise be ignorant of affairs affecting thousands across the world?"

Hathach, taken aback, had no ready answer, and was about to repeat the queen's command when Mordecai rose to his feet and grasped him by the arm.

Hundreds watched in silent admiration as their hero guided Hathach across the court, talking all the while about what had transpired between himself and Haman, and the exact amount of money offered by the treacherous prime minister in return for the lives of the Jews. Leading the bewildered fellow through the crowd until they stood before a public notice board, he turned him about to face the masses.

Then, reaching for the hideous parchment which had been posted that noon, he ripped it from the billboard and waved it beneath the eunuch's aquiline nose.

"Here!" he shouted. "Take this to the queen, and read it to her. Plead her forgiveness for the embarrassment heaped upon her, for the hypocrisy which expects her to rule without knowledge!"

Hathach, face red, tried to stammer some defense, but Mordecai would hear none.

"When you are done explaining this horror to the queen," the Jew demanded, "charge her to go to the king, to entreat Xerxes on behalf of these folk and to supplicate for their lives!"

Charge the queen? Such a notion was unthinkable.

But Mordecai, seeing Hathach's hesitation, shouted again as he walked away, "Our blood be upon you, and upon Our Lady, if you do not what I say!"

Stumbling across the congested pavement, Hathach scurried toward the palace, eager to be free of the mocking throng.

In his hand was the parchment, tightly crimped and awaiting the queen's scrutiny. As he disappeared behind the golden doors, the crowd's laughter turned once more to chanting, the name of Mordecai heralding the emergence of the moon.

40

Esther stood upon her balcony, listening to the chants which rose from the distant courtyard. She could not see the people who by blood were her kindred and who wrestled with the fate mapped for them. But she shared their agony, for she too faced the possibility of death.

Tears glimmered along her lashes as she turned a small parchment over and over in her fingers. It was a letter from Mordecai, and its contents bore the gravest challenge of her young life—a prospect even more frightening than eternal imprisonment within these palace walls.

To Mordecai's plea that she entreat the king on behalf of the Jews, she had sent word reminding him that no one could go into the king's court without his personal summons. Not even she, his queen, could do so without risking execution. Only if he were to extend his golden scepter to her might she be received. And though most would expect that she, of all people, would be welcomed into his presence, she had neither seen nor been requested by her husband for 30 days.

All this she had told Mordecai. But perhaps he had not believed her. Who could believe, having not heard her last conversation with Xerxes? The royal couple's most intimate servants had doubtless noted the distance between the king and his bride. But likely they assumed he had simply tired of her, that the growing harem was of more interest these days.

Esther, however, knew the true reason for her husband's aloofness. She knew he had been pained by her rejection, and that the rebuff merited his regal indignation. Indeed, it was a wonder he had borne the humiliation so calmly.

In her brief reply to Mordecai she had revealed none of this.

But as she surveyed his response, she knew it would have made no difference.

"Think not that just because you are in the king's palace you will escape," was his unwavering directive. "If you keep silent, deliverance will rise for the Jews from another place, but you and your father's house will perish."

The warning stung her, forbidding all complacency. *Had* she come to trust in her newfound privileges? *Had* the station into which she had been thrust become less than loathsome to her?

Gazing about at the fine furnishings of her boudoir, she shook herself. Mordecai's injunction had drawn the knife of conscience, making her cringe beneath its exposing gleam.

"No," she asserted. "I am *Hadassah*."

The name still felt at home upon her tongue, and she knew she still loved her heritage. Always she had been Israel's child. Why, even her challenge to Xerxes had come from a heart miserably entrapped within these Persian walls.

To others she was Queen of the East. To herself she was yet Hadassah.

Still, fear was her companion. Her defense to Mordecai had been fitly framed. She *would* be taking her life in her hands to step unbidden into the emperor's stateroom.

Trembling, she listened to the chants pushing up from the courtyard. Fumbling once again with the parchment, she contemplated its closing words.

"Who knows," it said, "but what you have come to the kingdom for such a time as this?"

For such a time as this . . .

The phrase beckoned, repeating itself over and over.

As though it were yesterday, she recalled her conversation with her papa when he had first met her in the harem hall.

"Jehovah has brought you to this place," he had deduced. "Trust everything to God."

How she had hated those words at the time! But now, telescoping into the present, all the unthinkable events which had led to this moment seemed suddenly capable of interpretation.

Perhaps, after all, she had been drawn into Persia's royal life for a high purpose—a purpose far greater than that of being queen. Perhaps she could be a servant—savior of her people.

A quiver of awe thrilled through her. Hardly did she feel worthy of such an assignment.

But as the chants outside grew more insistent, she suddenly raised her chin. Wheeling about, she clapped for a maid, sending her off to find a scribe.

And when the scribe arrived, she gave quick instruction. "Draft a note to Mordecai the Jew," she commanded. "Tell him to gather together all the Jews of Susa, that they may fast for me. They must neither eat nor drink for three days and nights. I and my maids will also fast. Then I will go in unto the king, which is against the law. And if I perish . . . I perish."

ESTHER

PART VI
The Triumph

41

Esther the Queen left her chamber in the strength of prayer. Robed in purple, her royal crown upon her head, she stepped into the hallway for the first time in three days.

Early she had risen, calling for her maids to prepare her bath, and eagerly they had complied, having been denied access to Her Majesty and having done her no service since her meditations had begun. Bewildered, the maids had filled their time in trivial employments during the queen's self-imposed isolation. They did not understand her ordeal of private prayer, or her command that they fast for three days along with her. They knew she prayed for the Jews, who still chanted in the public square. But her seemingly inordinate concern for their welfare was a mystery.

Esther had kept her devotions private, just as she kept her race and her faith a secret. Her servants did not know the God to whom she prayed, and so she had faced this test alone.

Now, however, as she emerged from her cloister decked in regal attire, her face barely showing the strain of hunger and fatigue, folk gathered about her in amazement.

Dorca was there, as well as Hegai, waiting in the hall and worrying. Her seven chambermaids, her devoted friend Maryam, and countless palace servants clustered in the corridor, gazing upon her and restraining the questions which hammered to be spoken.

"Your Highness," Dorca said with a bow, "we are so pleased to see you! We have been gravely concerned, My Lady, for your welfare."

"I am fine," the queen replied, smiling, her chin lifted in a determined angle. "I have been upheld by the prayers of many people."

The plump servant studied her vaguely, wondering at the statement. Whispers passed among those gathered.

"But I have one request of you," Esther added.

"Anything, Your Majesty!" Dorca replied, her face radiant.

"Prepare a table in my dining room. Three wine goblets and a carafe of fine wine."

"Yes, Your Majesty," the servant said, squelching her curiosity.

No one asked the reason for this assignment, nor for the queen's monastic behavior during the past days. It was not proper to question royalty. But when Esther lifted her skirts and turned toward the king's stateroom, a murmur of fascination, and then of fear, filled the onlookers.

"His Majesty is in his receiving hall, is he not?" she inquired.

At this Hegai drew near, his face white.

"He is, My Lady," he answered furtively. "Always on the third day of the week . . ."

"Very well," Esther nodded. And with a placid countenance she continued on her way.

"But, My Queen . . ." the eunuch objected.

"I am well," Esther assured him.

Passing through vestibule and lobby, she attracted a train of awed followers, but offered no further consolation.

* * *

Esther stood outside the emperor's audience hall, the elegant Apadana, whose princely columns, though 36 in number, were so narrow of girth that they barely intruded upon the vast space.

As the airy lightness of the stateroom collided with the shadow of the outer court, the queen's tamed fears clawed to assert themselves. At her back a dozen personal aides pleaded that she reconsider.

"Your Highness," they reminded her, "you know the penalty . . ."

"I know," she insisted. Walking up to the guards at the stateroom door, she stood silently, peering between their spears.

Beyond, she could see her husband seated upon his throne, a ledger of appointments in his hand, and his seven aides at his side.

"Our Lady," one of the guards whispered, his spear quivering in a sweaty hand as he recognized her intentions. "Do you mean to enter here?"

For a long moment Esther said nothing, only studying Xerxes as he casually chatted with his valets.

"I do," she replied at last, taking a deep breath.

Glancing at his fellow guard, the sentinel hesitated, feeling that to raise his long weapon and admit the queen was tantamount to decreeing her death.

But his partner, nervously complying, warned him with a look that they must obey their lady's wishes.

Ever so slowly they turned their spears upright, allowing Esther to step into the stateroom light. Fearing for their lady's safety, they could not bring themselves to announce her, but only stood aside like impotent shadows.

Silent as a statue she stood, waiting for the emperor to look upon her. Her pulse counted the minutes with a stammer, as her life hung on the king's response.

It was Mehuman, the chief eunuch, who at last spied the queen standing at the edge of the court. Eyes wide, he turned to his master and whispered in his ear.

Lurching erect, the emperor stared across the room, puzzled at the sight of his wife.

The instant Xerxes saw her, Esther lowered her head and bowed in a deep curtsy, her knees nearly touching the floor, a gesture befitting a queen only in deference to her husband. And for a long while she held this position, not daring to glance up, her heart drumming.

As the eunuchs conferred together, wondering at the woman's motives, the king only leaned forward in amazement, studying his daring bride.

Beautiful she was, in her courage, in her humility—as beautiful as ever he had seen her. How she reminded him, again, of Vashti—not only in appearance but in spirit!

His hand tightened upon the arm of his chair as he recalled, as though it were yesterday, the night his first queen had challenged him. Her self-assertion had exiled her as he in his pride had retaliated.

Once again, a lovely woman was laying her very life at his feet. But this time he could not imagine the purpose.

As he pondered the mystery, however, an explanation much to his liking suddenly dawned upon him. Perhaps, his fond heart told him, perhaps Esther, heartsick at his monthlong rejection of her, had come to plead for his husbandly attentions. Yes, he counseled himself, the love she had experienced in his kingly arms must have been a treasure sorely missed. Indeed, she regretted her unkind words when last they met. Life had lost all meaning without him, and therefore was worth risking, if only he might be hers again.

As he considered the countless females whom he had spurned, the harem wenches and concubines who had lain with him only once, forever after to live in solitary widowhood, a glib smile pricked his lips.

Lifting a hand, he reached for his scepter, and Mehuman, who had witnessed his abuse of Vashti, handed it to him fearfully. The eunuch knew that whatever Xerxes did with the royal wand would decide Esther's fate. If the emperor thumped the floor with the scepter's foot, the queen would die. If he extended it, she would live. Not having a clue to the king's heart, Mehuman quietly joined his brethren behind the throne.

Whether it was compassion for this lady, or guilt at the remembrance of Vashti, not even Xerxes could have said. But something softened his despotic nature as he gazed upon the queen. Her loveliness alone could have worked the miracle. But more than physical winsomeness worked for her this day.

When the monarch raised the golden shaft, a hush thrilled through the court. And when he extended it, pointing the glistening head toward his queen, a great sigh of relief ascended.

Scarcely believing what her ears told her, Esther found strength to lift her head. Tears nudged at her lashes as she saw the beckoning orb. Rising, she crossed the room, bowing again when she reached the throne, and touched the scepter's top with careful fingers.

"What is it, Queen Esther?" Xerxes said, his heart pounding now as the gentle woman stood before him. A quaver of manly emotion colored his tone as he proclaimed, "What is your request? It shall be given you, even to half of my kingdom."

Standing, Esther smiled. But though he tried desperately, Xerxes could not interpret her feelings.

"If it please the king," she replied, her voice sweet and supple, "let the king and Haman come this day to a dinner that I have prepared."

Quizzically, Xerxes sank back upon his throne. Haman? Why Haman?

But of course, he reasoned, she was being coy. She would win him cautiously, in the presence of another.

Not taking his eyes off her, he gave a condescending nod. Flicking a careless hand toward Mehuman, he commanded, "Fetch Haman quickly, that we may do as Esther desires."

At this the queen curtsied again and backed away from the king's platform. Turning, she hastened toward the door.

Smitten by the woman's self-possession, the emperor watched her departure. When she disappeared from sight, he shook his head, chuckling with delight.

42

Haman doffed his leather skullcap to every servant, every chambermaid, every doorman as he sidled through the palace halls, his head light with wine and his heart merry. Smugly smiling to himself, he reveled in the irony of the honor just heaped upon him.

How Otanes would laugh with him when Haman told him he had just come from dinner in the queen's hall! He, Haman, coconspirator for the death of Xerxes, had just sat at private banquet with the emperor and his lady. He who had only recently been publicly elevated, obliging obeisance from all who saw him, had now been received by the queen—an award only rarely bestowed. In fact, he could not recall such an honor ever being given a palace official during Darius' reign or since.

Not only this, but he had been invited to dine with the royal couple again tomorrow evening! The prestige was almost more than he could bear.

He could not imagine what he had done to deserve either invitation. He could accept the thought that he was a stunning fellow, brilliant and charming. Perhaps this was enough. And perhaps, he snickered, not even his plan to overthrow the king could be thwarted.

His step lively, he ambled through the court on his way home, recalling with fond satisfaction the luxuries of Esther's hall. How lovely the queen had been! Reclined upon her dinner couch, her linen gown the same lavender as the lounge's linen upholstery, her hair and eyes black as the marble tiles bordering her porch—she was a memorable sight.

The conversation had been airy and carefree. Matters of state did not intrude as the empress spoke of the weather and asked caring questions about his wife and family.

Proudly he had told her of his ten sons, and if her eyes darkened at this, he knew not why, nor did he notice.

Toward Xerxes she had shown the same casual ease. Haman had not attempted to interpret her feelings toward her husband. Her gracious hospitality toward himself was all he absorbed.

His blood glowed with the wine's caress as he headed toward the palace door, eager to share his good fortune with plump and comely Zeresh, his wife of a quarter-century.

But just as he entered the outer porch, near the king's gate, the chanting of the Jews in the public square reached his ears, and a chill ran through his veins.

Ahead sat Mordecai. Having removed his sackcloth and having washed himself, he had taken his station behind his accounting desk. Though it was night, he had perched himself there, awaiting Haman's emergence. And the instant the prime minister saw him, Mordecai's eyes locked on his with a knowing twinkle.

When the Jew neither rose nor trembled before him, Haman seethed with indignation.

Restraining himself, he passed by without a word. But his glorious day had been ruined. Utterly ruined.

* * *

Haman entered his house with a bowed head. Zeresh, who had eagerly anticipated his homecoming all evening, rushed to him with open arms. But seeing the dark cloud upon his face, she faltered.

"My Lord," she fawned, stroking him on the shoulder and removing his cape with solicitous hands, "I trust it went well— your dinner with the queen."

"Call Otanes," was all he could say. "Call my friends, my confidants."

Bewildered, Zeresh would have inquired more deeply, but knowing her husband's determined personality, she hastened to comply. Sending her servants through the neighborhood, she saw to it that all her husband's associates were summoned, and then she sat with him by the fire to await their arrival.

"It did not go well?" she managed.

"I will tell the tale when I have an audience," he curtly corrected, though Zeresh probed his expression for further clues.

Shortly the house filled with Haman's executives, who gathered doubtfully, wondering why they were required to leave home and hearth at so late an hour.

When at last Otanes arrived, seating himself across from Haman's ten sons, the grand vizier began to pace the floor.

"You are all aware of the honor I received this day . . . that I did dine with the emperor and his wife in the queen's hall," he said.

Murmurs and nodding heads confirmed this.

Then, with dramatic tears in his eyes, he recounted the trophies of his life.

"You all know that I am a wealthy man, that no one in the kingdom surpasses me for financial security."

Again, everyone agreed, though not without resentment.

"I have fathered ten sons!" he cried, throwing his arms wide, and caressing his heirs with proud scrutiny.

Zeresh beamed, and Haman's friends condoled that this was indeed true. The fact that they did not feel as much warmth for their superior as he imagined would not trouble him.

"Furthermore," he went on, "everyone knows how I have been honored by His Majesty . . . his public endorsements of me . . . the promotions I have received in sight of all the empire!"

Heedless of his associates' growing uneasiness, he did not consider the affront which Otanes might feel at this self-aggrandizement. Nor did the memory of Otanes' personal involvement in his "promotion" faze him.

"Why," he boasted, "I have been advanced above all the princes and servants of the king! Even Queen Esther let no one come with the king to the banquet but me!"

Any applause now elicited was given only out of duty. But Haman accepted it with condescension.

"And tomorrow also I am invited to dine with the queen and king! Yet . . ."

Here he paused, his voice cracking and his face falling.

"Yet . . . all this does me no good as long as I see Mordecai the Jew sitting at the king's gate!"

At this Zeresh stood and rushed to his side, begging him to seat himself, to calm his heart lest it break.

After a hesitant moment, one by one the advisers began to console him.

"Truly, Master," they sympathized, "this monster, Mordecai, would be a thorn in any man's side. Such patience you have shown in enduring his insults!"

Haman kept his head bowed, gazing into the fire with contorted countenance. But how he loved their forced support!

For a long while Otanes studied his partner in crime. He had no great love for Haman. In fact, he despised the pompous braggart. But Haman was the most useful pawn to the general's vendetta against Xerxes. The prime minister's recent intimacies with the royal family could only hasten the fulfillment of Otanes' plot. If Mordecai were dampening Haman's spirit, he must be done away with.

A cold-blooded warrior, one who enjoyed the sport of power, Otanes would just as soon kill a man as put up with any inconvenience he might pose.

His voice smooth as honey, he called Haman's name and crossed the room, embracing Zeresh as though he treasured her. "Dear friends," he began, "I cannot express the sorrow I have at the sight of your discomfort. I think we all agree that this is a serious matter, calling for immediate action. For you, Haman, are our brother as well as our superior."

No one dared deny this as syrupy smiles graced each conciliatory face.

"Therefore, after due consideration, I have a plan which, with your indulgence, Prime Minister, I will address."

Haman glanced sideways at Otanes. Feigning deference, he bowed.

"Let a gallows 50 cubits high be built," Otanes coolly suggested. "And in the morning, tell the king to have Mordecai hanged upon it. Then go merrily with Xerxes to the dinner."

How simply the matter had been resolved! How easily death became the answer!

Here and there a face went white, but no one spoke contrary to Otanes.

Zeresh, her lips wet, planted a firm kiss on Haman's wan cheek.

"Oh, my husband!" she cried. "Heed our beloved Otanes! Free yourself of this plague, of the cloud which hangs over you, and be our merry Haman once again!"

Nothing but endorsement issued from the little gathering. Haman had his answer—an answer which set well with his callous spirit.

"Thank you, friends," he smiled, a polished tear reflecting firelight on his face. "It shall be done."

43

That night Xerxes found sleep impossible to achieve. Each time he came near dozing, the sight of Esther, gracefully reclined upon her dinner bed, invaded his masculine heart.

He had never thought of her as a seductress. She had not needed to play such games with him. But he was certain that today's invitation to the dinner, given at peril of her own life, was an attempt to woo him. Even buffering the encounter with the presence of a third party, Haman, was doubtless part of her strategy.

How coolly she had handled things during the rendezvous, focusing more on Haman than on himself—asking all those idle questions about the vizier's career and family, chitchatting about the weather and the delicacies of the table!

Certainly her tactics were effective. She had captivated him, and his thoughts had been on her alone all evening.

Wide awake, he paced his room, glancing out at the desert moon over and over. Thoughts of Vashti and thoughts of Esther blended into one, as always they had done since the girl had come to him. Deep inside he knew that Esther's accusation of him had been valid—that he saw his first wife in her more than he saw herself. But perhaps today's encounter had been her way of telling him that she could live with the fact. That she would take him—indeed, craved him—regardless.

As he stepped onto his balcony with the dawn, having paced and tossed and turned all night, a strange sound, intermittent and persistent, intruded upon his reveries. It seemed to be a hammering of some kind, as though a construction job were underway upon the acropolis.

Generally Susa was quiet at such an early hour. Though the labyrinth of palace corridors and walls could deflect vibrations at misleading angles, he was sure the pounding came from the direction of Haman's house. As he cocked his head to listen, he noticed that the odd chanting which had filled the public square for days and nights had ceased, as though the hammering had replaced it.

Persians could be a hot-blooded race, and the many diverse nationalities comprising Susa were a volatile combination. Protests or sit-ins were not a rare sight in the public market. Xerxes had not bothered to ask just what the most recent discontent regarded. If it concerned his edict against Haman's alleged foes of the state, he knew it would pass. After all, he was certain the accused people must be only a minute fraction of the population, having done nothing to attract his attention before Haman clued him to their subversion.

Glad he was that his prime minister was so in touch with the citizens. Surely no king could have a more efficient adviser.

But glad he would also be to sleep.

In times past he would have called for one of his harem girls to distract him, to soothe his body and tire him enough for slumber. Now, however, he would have been content with no one but Esther. And he knew the timing was not right to have her. She must play out her winsome plan, and he must indulge her scheme.

Meanwhile, as his heart drummed to thoughts of her, and as the mysterious hammers chattered through the twilight, he grew irritable.

Clapping his hands, he called for Mehuman, who appeared the instant the guards opened the king's door.

"Mehuman!" Xerxes snapped. "What is that infernal pounding?"

"Hammers, Your Highness," the eunuch said with a bow.

"Of course it is!" the emperor growled. "I know it is hammers! But why—why at this hour?"

"Some project of Haman's, Your Majesty," Mehuman replied. "A gallows of immense proportions. I am certain he will inform you . . ."

"Yes, yes. Very well," Xerxes nodded, raising a limp hand to his throbbing temple. "I have not slept all night."

Mehuman, whose duty it was to anticipate the emperor's every need, quickly offered to send word commanding quiet in the acropolis. But Xerxes only quipped, "It would do no good now, since the night is already gone. My spirit is restless."

"Perhaps, Your Highness, if someone read to you . . ."

Xerxes had suffered often from insomnia, especially since sending Vashti away, and sometimes his troubled mind was calmed if someone lulled him with a reading.

His tired eyes brightening, the king grasped at the idea.

"Send for the Book of Memorable Deeds," he cried. "Yes, yes . . . I do enjoy that!"

He referred, as Mehuman knew, to the royal chronicles, a scrupulously maintained record of all the valorous and complimentary things done in the empire by folk of all stations. If a general pulled off an amazing feat in battle, if a commoner performed some especially heroic act, if an inventor notably contributed to the empire's technology, or if a physician advanced the cause of medicine by discovering some valued cure— any such achievement would be noted in the chronicle.

Of particular honor were acts of benevolence directed toward the king's personal welfare. And periodically Xerxes enjoyed being updated as to the contents.

Two scribes appeared quickly with the priceless volume, bowing through the door. To the monarch's delight, they began to recount the story of how a certain Jew had once saved the emperor's life.

"Mordecai, you say?" Xerxes mused. "Of course, I remember. He revealed the plot of my treacherous guards, Bigthan and Teresh!"

"Yes, Sire," the readers confirmed. "It says here that he reported the scheme to your queen, and she to you."

Xerxes' eyes again brightened at the thought of his wife. And fondly he contemplated the tale of Mordecai.

"He is a palace accountant?"

"Head of inventory," the scribes reminded him.

"And what honor or dignity has been bestowed on Mordecai for this kindness?"

The readers scanned the pages, their fingers tracing the scroll line by line.

At last, shrugging, they replied, "Nothing has been done for him."

* * *

Somewhere beyond the palace wall a morning cock crowed.
And with the twilight, hastening footsteps rang through the king's receiving hall.

"Who is in the court?" Xerxes asked as he sat upon his stateroom throne. To his right, on a low table, sat the Book of Memorable Deeds, and upon his lap was a roster of items to be considered this day, judgments to be made, and visitors to be entertained.

"Haman is here, Your Majesty, asking to see you," Mehuman replied.

"Good, good," Xerxes smiled. "Let him come in." Then, glancing at the book of deeds, he enthused, "I could use his advice!"

Promptly Haman entered, eager to speak to the king regarding his planned execution of Mordecai, and ready for the quick consent which was always given his wishes. When the emperor interrupted him with a spirited inquiry, he was caught off guard.

"Good morning, friend," Xerxes called as Haman approached. "What shall be done to the man whom the king delights to honor?"

Assuming that this was a mere pleasantry, Haman only bowed. But when the king repeated the question, the vizier gave it more thought. Of course Xerxes must be referring to the prime minister himself. Whom, after all, would the emperor delight to honor more than himself? Had not Xerxes already heaped acclaim and dignity upon him? It seemed there was no limit to the king's generosity toward those he loved.

Haman cleared his throat. "Why, Sire," he chuckled, feigning embarrassment, "for such a man let royal robes be brought, which the king has worn, and the horse which the king has ridden, on whose head a royal crown is set." Gaining more boldness with each selfish syllable, he continued, "And let the robes and the horse be handed over to one of the king's most noble princes. Let him array the man whom the king delights to honor, and let him conduct the man on horseback through the open square of the city, proclaiming before him, 'Thus shall it be done to the man whom the king delights to honor!' "

Leaning back on his throne, Xerxes laughed with Haman. "Ah-hah!" he cried. "Marvelous! Make haste, my friend. Take the robes and the horse, as you have said, and do so to Mordecai the Jew who sits at the king's gate. Leave out nothing that you have mentioned."

44

There was no parade in the Susa streets, but folk from all quarters lined the viaduct before the king's palace. There was no military processional or train of acrobats and actors to draw a crowd. But thousands had turned out to observe two men's passage down the royal avenue.

The rumor of the king's command to Haman had spread through the palace court like wildfire, and by the time Mordecai had been summoned, an amazed throng awaited him.

When he appeared upon a white, prancing charger, upon whose noble head was set a shining tiara, the crowd was delighted. Mordecai himself was dressed in a blue gown of purest silk, his silver beard lying gloriously against it. Not only did Jews line the avenue, but supportive Susaites of all sorts. And when it was seen that *Haman* had been commissioned to parade the bookkeeper through town, hilarity was the order of the day.

In fact, the hilarity had begun at court, when Haman set about to fulfill the king's commission. Calling for Mordecai, he was obliged to deck the Jew, firsthand, in the royal apparel. Then, leading the regal horse to his enemy, he bowed in chagrin as the accountant mounted the beast.

Now, of course, his humiliation was unbounded as the thousands who had chanted hatred for him watched, hissing and spitting, while he conducted their hero through the streets.

Mortified, he kept his eyes to the ground as Mordecai was lauded, wondering how this irony had come to be, and how the man he had planned to execute on this very day could be his sudden superior.

When he reached the public square, he was obliged to make the pronouncement which he himself had ordained: "Thus shall it be done to the man whom the king delights to honor," he cried, his voice a rasping croak.

Over and over he shouted the words, until he thought his tongue would bleed for shame.

And all the while Mordecai said nothing, only reveling in the victory of Jehovah.

* * *

Zeresh swabbed her husband's perspiring brow with a damp cloth. Red-faced and close to weeping, he had come home with his head covered, not needing to tell his sorry tale, for his wife, along with all Suṣa, knew of his humiliation.

Nevertheless, the grisly details spilled forth in a torrent of shame and self-pity as he recounted to her, to his household servants, and to the advisers who lived on his estate the horrid events of the day.

"With my own hands I was obliged to drape the royal cloak about that scoundrel's shoulders!" he wailed. "With my own hand I was forced to lead him forth through the streets! Oh, my friends," he bellowed, "how shall I ever live it down?"

Zeresh tried to calm him, but it was no use. One by one his counselors, who had themselves encouraged him to take vengeance against the Jew, offered worthless comfort.

"Lord," they reasoned, "surely Xerxes was unaware of your hatred for this man. Perhaps he did not even know Mordecai is a Jew. Had he known," they insisted, "he would never have elevated him."

Haman sank into his chair, shaking his head. He could not admit to his friends that Xerxes was unaware of more than this—that Xerxes did not even know that the edict so recently published against the "subversives" was against the entire Jewish race.

But as the counselors considered their master's unhappy state, another concern formed in their minds.

Whispering together, they contemplated a new side to the dilemma, and Haman, observing their knit brows, leaned forward anxiously.

"What is it?" he demanded.

"Uh, sir," one spoke, clearing his throat, "it occurs to us that your humiliation may only be beginning."

"How so?" he inquired.

"Why," the adviser said softly, "if Mordecai, before whom you have begun to fall, is of the Jewish people, and if Xerxes knows this, the king may begin to side with the Jews. And you will not prevail against Mordecai, but will surely fall utterly."

The possibilities were too horrible to contemplate. Loss of influence, perhaps even of position . . . or of life . . .

When Xerxes began to put all the facts together, seeing that Haman had no just cause for the edict, there would be no salvation!

Quaking, Zeresh drew close to her husband and cried, "They are right, of course! How can you stand before the king?"

But there was no time for answers. At that instant messengers from the palace arrived at the mansion, summoning Haman to the feast prepared in Esther's hall.

Turning helplessly to his wife, Haman stood on shaky legs as Zeresh handed him his cloak and studied him with mournful eyes.

Feeling as though he were headed for his own execution, the man who had just last night commissioned a gallows left the house.

45

Today's banquet was even more festive than yesterday's, confounding Haman.

If he had been confused by Xerxes' commission to heap honor upon Mordecai, he now began to suspect that the king and Esther were playing games with him.

Yet if it was a game he had no choice but to play along—to hope that his past status as the king's favorite would carry him above the mixed messages he was receiving. He must not mention the morning's humiliation. He must draw no further attention to Mordecai, in conversation or in attitude, lest the king pursue the issue.

Perhaps, after all, Haman was still the emperor's most esteemed prince. Perhaps the incident with Mordecai was a fluke, and his own fears were unfounded.

Stretching his lips into a smile, he followed the messengers into the queen's hall. He tried not to register surprise at the sumptuous array upon the long table, or at the elegant decor which had been lavished on the place. Yet it was evident that Esther had spared no expense in making the room and the meal even more luxurious than yesterday's feast, surrounding the little gathering with immense bouquets and calling all her servants to serve.

As he bowed to the royal couple—the king, who sat upon a high pile of ornate pillows, and the queen, who reclined majestically upon her couch—his chest ached with anxiety. When he took his own seat, he hesitated to study their faces.

What he saw when he did so gave no clue to their view of him. Xerxes, after a cheery greeting, seemed to focus all attention on his queen, so that Haman began to wonder if his presence were a hindrance to their bliss. Esther, on the other hand, attended to Haman with a persistence which made him equally uneasy.

Not once did she allow his cup to run dry or his plate to go bare. Not once did the conversation lag, though he sensed a peculiar scrutiny in her eyes and an ironic lilt to her voice.

Just as he was thinking he might enjoy her attentions, however, Xerxes drew her away.

Hoisting a fluted goblet, the king toasted his lady's beauty. Then, almost groaning, he suddenly declared, "What is your petition, Queen Esther? It shall be granted you! And what is your request? It shall be given you, even to half of my kingdom!"

Servants ceased their serving, slaves lowered pitcher-laden trays from their shoulders, and the men who guarded the chamber stood rigid with surprise.

Such a statement made by a king was not unheard of. Xerxes had spoken this very thing to Esther yesterday. It was usually reserved for those who had performed some great feat in service to the empire, and it was never to be taken literally. Still, it was an incomparable honor, and to be spoken twice in two days to a woman, even to a queen, made it even more noteworthy.

If the offer were amazing, however, so would be the queen's response. No one anticipated that she would so boldly pursue Xerxes' generosity—not the king himself nor any of the onlookers.

Esther felt a flush rise to her cheeks, and every fiber of her being tingled with the opportunity afforded.

Hammered and honed by palace life into a female of power and prestige, Esther was no longer the meek Jewess who had been dragged into the harem. A few weeks earlier she had boldly confronted her "husband" with his unfair use of herself and Vashti. Then, wielding the weapon of faith, she had risked her life to enter his stateroom, seeking help (unbeknownst to him) for her people.

Now in a compulsive moment he had fulfilled her deepest longing, unwittingly granting her the chance to attain salvation for the Jews.

As she studied the floor, framing in her mind just how to speak her wish, Xerxes wondered at the interlude.

Indeed, he had opened the world to Esther with a few words. But surely she must not make so much of it! Was she so unschooled in Persian protocol that she knew not the typical response? Would she not simply smile and calmly thank his lordship, fawning over the treasures of her chamber and the glories of his love? Would she not simply say that she had everything a woman could ask, and that to receive more would overwhelm her?

Still, she pondered her answer until even the servants grew embarrassed. Then, as she turned scalding eyes on Haman, boring through him with a vengeful stare, whispers filled the room.

At last, tears trickling down her hot cheeks, she slid from her couch and fell to her knees, burying her face in her hands.

"Oh, My Lord!" she cried. "If I have found favor in your sight, O King, and if it please the king, let my life be given me at my petition, and my people at my request! For we are sold, I and my people, to be destroyed, to be slain, and to perish. If we had been sold into slavery, I would have kept silent, for such a thing would not be worthy of the king's attention."

Unprepared for this strange turn of events, Xerxes beheld his lady with amazement. "Of what do you speak, my dear?" he marveled.

The queen, rocking back on her heels, at last revealed her long-kept secret. "I am a Jewess," she declared, "the daughter of Mordecai, whom you have honored this day. But I and all my people live in fear for their lives!"

"Who would do such a thing?" the king demanded, scowling about the room. "Where is he?"

Esther leaped to her feet, abandoned now to the liberty of the moment, and pointed a revenging finger at their guest. "A foe and an enemy!" she cried. "This wicked Haman!"

Utterly bewildered, Xerxes digested the accusation, his volatile nature seething with indignation. So, Haman had pressed an edict against an entire race, even to the life of his own queen!

Rising from his bolsters, the emperor glowered down upon the cringing vizier. No word escaped his lips, but his countenance was livid. With a clenched fist he stalked from the banquet hall, exiting into the adjacent garden.

Mortified, Haman turned to the queen, his own face now covered with tears. Esther, having returned to her couch, scorned to look upon him until he, a crazed fool, threw himself at her feet.

"Oh, Your Majesty," he wailed, "Take mercy upon me. Speak unto the king on my behalf, My Lady, I beg of you! For my life surely is in your hands!"

When Esther only recoiled, drawing her skirts up from the floor, he grew even more desperate. In an attitude of utmost despair he scrambled toward her, flinging himself across her dinner bed and weeping like one of the damned.

"Will he even assault the queen before my very eyes?" Xerxes shouted, reentering from the garden. At this the eunuchs scurried forth, draping Haman's head with a cloth for shame, and dragging him into the center of the room.

There he sat, rocking to and fro, wailing like a skewered hog, until Harbona, one of the king's attendants, reminded Xerxes of the gallows which Haman had built only the previous night.

" . . . made for Mordecai, who saved the king's life!" he revealed.

"No, you cannot mean it!" Xerxes spat.

"Indeed, it is so," Harbona declared. "This fiend would have killed the Jew for no matter greater than his own pride."

Even in his escapades against the Greeks, when he would have taken the Western world, Xerxes had never felt a desire for revenge more strongly than he did this moment.

Pointing a spasmed finger at the cowering Haman, he roared vindictive judgment.

"Hang him on it!" he commanded.

With this the guards hurried forth, jolting Haman to his feet and carrying him from the room. Xerxes, his face contorted with bombarding emotions, took Esther's hand, lifting her to his bosom and holding her close to his heart.

46

"Oh, Papa! How wonderful you look!" Esther declared, studying her adopted father's reflection in her hallway mirror. "A more distinguished fellow has never come before the king's throne!"

Mordecai gazed upon his dapper likeness, not concealing a broad smile. For his daughter had just draped about his shoulders a robe once belonging to the king. And his tunic, given him only yesterday by Haman, was the one he had worn as the prime minister led him through the Susa streets.

"Are you not splendid?" Esther laughed. "I am proud of you, Papa!"

Mordecai turned about, grasping the queen's hands. "Why has the king called for me?" he wondered. "Has he not already honored me?"

Esther perceived his anxiety at the notion of standing before the despot. Trying to reassure him, she nodded, "Xerxes has his gentle side, Papa. And he is very generous, once he takes a liking to someone."

"And swift to retribution when someone crosses him," he added, remembering the vizier's quick demise.

Hung on the gallows prepared for Mordecai, Haman had met his death only last evening. And just as quickly, at the king's command, the dead man's house and all his wealth had passed to Queen Esther.

"But in his eyes, Papa, you are a hero. You once saved his life. Remember?"

"I have sometimes questioned the wisdom . . ." he grinned.

"Hush, Papa," Esther giggled, glancing warily down the hall. "Now, come! He waits for you!"

As the bookkeeper entered the lobby, the king's eunuchs stood ready to receive him. Hastening, they took the queen and her adopted father to the stateroom.

The reception would be quiet this time, but very dignified. When Xerxes, seated upon his throne, had extended his scepter to the couple in the presence of all his princes and advisers, he stretched forth his open palm, upon which was perched his signet ring.

"This I took from the hand of your enemy, Haman," Xerxes explained. "It is my own ring of law, by which your enemy did seal the death of your people. So now receive this, my friend, as a token of apology, and in honor of your kindness to me."

Mordecai stared mutely at the gift, hardly daring to consider the implications. Glancing at his daughter, who only nodded enthusiastically, he at last reached out and took it.

"Behold, my new prime minister!" Xerxes announced, gesturing toward the humble Jew with a dramatic sweep of the hand.

Trumpets blared and applause rang through the court. But scarcely could Mordecai believe his ears until Esther herself bowed before him.

Rising, she took from one of the king's aides a small pillow upon which was the key to Haman's house.

"With the emperor's approval, Father, I pass the wealth of your enemy into your keeping," she declared, placing the cushion on his hesitant hands.

Again celebration filled the air.

Wonderful as all this was, however, the queen's heart was not wholly joyous. She must speak again, and that without delay.

Turning to her master, she appealed to his generous mood, falling to her knees and releasing all the pent-up stress of past days.

"O My Lord," she cried, "surely the good you have done this day is only the beginning of your kindnesses. My people still fear for their lives due to the edict of Haman!"

Xerxes had known she would address this matter. He was learning to anticipate her bravery.

Extending to her his scepter once again, he bade her rise and speak her mind.

Smoothing her linen gown, she phrased her words with care, words rehearsed in the night.

"If it please the king, and if I have found favor in his sight, and if the thing seem right before the king, and I be pleasing in his eyes," she began, "let an order be written to revoke the letters devised by Haman the Agagite, the son of Hammedatha, which he wrote to destroy the Jews who are in all the provinces of the king. For how can I endure to see the destruction of my kindred?"

Her concentration on this little speech was so deliberate that she dare not contemplate the emperor's face until she was done. But when she at last allowed reflection, she found his countenance soft toward her.

In his eyes was the warmth of love, and she cared not now how genuine.

"Behold," he addressed both Esther and her father, his own voice husky with feeling, "I have given Esther the house of Haman, and have hanged him on the gallows, because he would lay hands on the Jews. And you may write as you please with regard to the Jews, in the name of the king, and sealed with the king's ring. For an edict written in the name of the king and sealed with the king's ring cannot be revoked."

47

Esther stood once again at her chamber window, where so much agonized prayer for her people had been lifted. She turned over in her hands a piece of parchment similar to the one on which Mordecai had challenged her to go before the king.

This paper, like that one, bore the handwriting of her papa, but these words were not for her eyes alone. They would be duplicated by countless scribes and sent to all parts of the empire, for they were the first edict of the new prime minister.

Persians were fond of saying that the laws of their kings, sealed with the royal signet ring, were irrevocable. But no dynastic ruler who reigned over half the world could truly be subject to such a restriction. While no subordinate official nor any uprising of the people could revoke an emperor's command, the emperor could not be his own slave.

Out of deference to his image, however, Esther and Mordecai had worded the new edict to accommodate the original. They would not do away with the planned day of assault against the Jews, but would instead send word throughout the empire telling the Jews to arm themselves.

Of course, there was more behind their decision to do this than honor for the king.

Esther felt a chill crawl up her arms as she dwelt on Mordecai's reasoning. All her life he had raised her in the ways of Israel. But tonight, for the first time, he had shared with her the tale told by Abihail, her departed father—the story of King Saul and the wicked foe, Agag.

"I thought Abihail was a foolish old man when first he spoke of the ancient tale," Mordecai had said. "But now that we have seen the wickedness which Haman devised against our people, I know that Saul was remiss in not stamping out the Amalekites."

Amazed, Esther had listened to the story, overwhelmed with the personal involvement of God in her own life. "So," she had replied carefully, "are you saying that Jehovah is using us now to right that wrong done so many years ago?"

At this Mordecai had risen from the queen's desk, where he had been penning the edict, and had gazed out the night window. Far away his mind was carried to the land of Israel and the distant time of King Saul his own ancestor.

"God never lets His purposes go unfulfilled," he answered softly. "All the world is hallowed ground, and years are of small consequence to Him. In His good time and in His chosen way He always brings about His will. Only we poor humans are bound by the frustrations of how and when."

"But why *me*?" Esther marveled. "Why has God chosen me, an orphan and a commoner, to perform this thing?"

Mordecai gazed lovingly into her awe-filled face.

"Why did He choose Rahab? Why Ruth? The women who mothered king David were of humble birth," he asserted. "Often God has raised up salvation for His people from the most unlikely places. Why," he mused, "who knows but what the mother of Messiah Himself shall be a girl of low station?"

Esther raised her hand to her mouth, stifling a giggle. And her papa, drawing her close, whispered, "Did I not tell you when you first came here to be anxious for nothing? Trust God, my dear Hadassah."

The last word had infused the young woman with zeal.

" 'Hadassah,' " she repeated. "I am still Hadassah, aren't I, Papa?"

"You never were anyone else," he assured her, bowing low and bidding good night.

That had been two hours ago. The queen should have been asleep long since. But, her heart still full of wakeful contemplation, she found sleep impossible.

The new edict, as Mordecai and she had agreed, would not only honor the king but would help to establish the people of God. While a simple revoking of Haman's command would have saved countless lives, the call to defense would secure the peace of the Jews by revealing who their enemies were, and who their friends. Like Saul should have done generations before, the Hebrews would now be able to stamp out their foes.

If the Jews were allowed to arm themselves, so would be their sympathizers. It had become quite obvious during the growing unrest over Haman's edict that there were many more who would side with Israel than not, given the opportunity. Mordecai's order would free them to aid their Jewish neighbors, and so the tables would be turned, resulting in a purge against the anti-Semites.

It seemed to Esther that she was being carried through these events on a supernatural wave—by a force outside herself. Never had she become accustomed to her role as queen. Perhaps, she thought, even that role was only a garment which she had donned for higher purposes. Inside, where her spirit dwelt, she was still a young girl standing at the village gate, tripping through the wheat fields, watching for her beloved David. And such memories lifted her above the present distress.

A knock at her door roused her from poignant reveries, and brushing a tear from her cheek, she went to answer it. In the hall's shadow stood her master, Xerxes, his ruddy face flushed with long-suppressed feeling.

"My Lady . . ." he whispered, bowing his head.

Esther's throat tightened. "It has been a long time, My Lord," she softly replied.

"Too long," Xerxes sighed. "May I come in?"

It occurred to Esther that this man could do as he pleased, entering and exiting at will through any door on earth. That he should humble himself in this way touched her.

Stepping away from the portal, she assented, but as he walked to her couch, removing his cloak and draping it over the foot, she hesitated to follow.

His gaze passed over the room, and she knew that, as always he thought of Vashti, who had once dwelt here. But his eyes fell on the parchment which Esther had set upon her desk, and for a moment she expected he might ask about the new edict.

Instead, however, he seemed to study her sadly, and she hoped he would not speak of love.

When he did begin to talk, she was surprised at the direction the conversation took.

"So," he said patting the seat beside him and bidding her draw near, "I have taken a Jewess to wife."

Esther nodded, sitting down. "Does this please or displease you?" she inquired.

"Nothing about you displeases me," he replied with a smile. "You are only a source of continual delight."

Esther blushed and looked away. It was not the blush of a virgin, for she was that no longer. Rather, it was the result of unvoiced longings, unmet needs.

"No," he went on, barely sensing her frustration, "I have nothing against the Jews. They are an odd lot, no doubt, but good people. And Mordecai is a popular man."

Then, reaching out, he touched her hand. "But I have not come for this, My Lady," he asserted tenderly. "Haven't you missed me all these weeks?"

Part of him still hoped that her recent advances toward him indicated more than a yearning to save her people, and he still dreamed she might crave his embrace.

Yet she was unyielding.

"You know, My King, that I have never belonged to you," she insisted, looking bravely into his face. "Since you know that I am a Jew, you must understand this now more than ever."

Something like a shudder passed through Xerxes as the long-avoided reality was addressed.

"And you have never truly been mine," she went on.

"This is not so," he objected. Then, more uncertainly, "Not so . . ."

Esther rose from the couch and stepped to the archway. For the first time he saw in her the attitude of the caged doe, of the wild thing in captivity, as she watched the distant fields and the dim-lit burgs of the peasants far beyond.

Xerxes was capable of sympathy. He was not an utterly heartless man. And he also knew, as he had known in Salamis, when he had lost and when to retreat.

"I could demand your love," he sighed, joining her at the window.

"No one can demand another's heart," Esther countered. "You have not even been able to force *yourself* to love *me*. Don't you see? It has all been a wicked game, My Lord, one which Jehovah has miraculously turned to His own ends."

Her tone was rising with her courage, but she caught herself short of disrespect. "My soul belongs to the God of Israel," she softened, "and my heart to yet another."

Xerxes bristled at these last words, his fists clenching. "Another? Do I know him?"

"He is a poor man, My King. Not mighty, not monied. But a prince nonetheless."

Xerxes would hear no more.

"What can I do?" he sighed. "I would give you anything . . . unto half my kingdom . . ."

For a long while their eyes locked on one another. Rigid body confronted rigid body until Esther dared reply.

"Let me go, then, My Lord. And restore Vashti to her rightful place."

Dumbfounded, Xerxes could say nothing. Was this child, this humble orphan girl, suggesting once more that he should reverse himself?

"You have the power, O King," she insisted. "Nothing is too hard for the Monarch of the World."

Possibilities swirled through Xerxes' head. But he resisted them. Had he not rejected Vashti? Had he not commanded a harem and slept with countless women since? Never could he bow to such humiliation as this slip of a female suggested.

Yet . . .

"If you reversed Haman's edict, sealed by your own signet ring, why cannot you do this?" Esther continued.

"Stop!" the king suddenly shouted. "How dare you . . ."

Gently, Esther drew near and took him by the hand.

"Follow your heart, Majesty. What is it you wish? You may have it with a word," she reminded him. "Or you may concede again, to pride, and lose all hope forever."

Staring at the floor, Xerxes stood with stooped shoulders. But gradually a smile conquered his downturned lips.

"Are all Jews as headstrong as you, my dear?" he asked.

"We are a stiff-necked people," she laughed. "A peculiar people."

Dawn was creeping over the Zagros. The king glanced toward the hazy realm of the East, and his heart seemed suddenly to drop its fetters.

"A glorious people!" he cried, sweeping the girl into his arms. "May your God be blessed, as you have blessed me, dear child!"

48

It was a time of fulfillment.

Such liberty and grace had not been experienced by the exiled Jews since their taking away into captivity, more than 200 years before. In a matter of two days, the thirteenth and fourteenth of Adar, the twelfth month of the year, the Jews had overcome their enemies.

Throughout Persia's vast empire, governors and deputies had risen to the aid of the "peculiar people," and those who had dared come out against them had been slain.

In Susa 800 enemies had been killed, testimony to the slim number who took such a stand and to the vindication of the Hebrew race. Elsewhere, over 75,000 met their deaths at the hands of the Jews and their sympathizers.

Even the ten sons of Haman had been destroyed, run through with Jewish swords, and then, at Esther's suggestion, hanged from the very gallows upon which their father had died.

"Let it be a testimony to the fulfillment of God's will," the queen had said. "Agag and his descendants are gone forever!"

Only the Jews could fully appreciate the meaning of this. And only they understood why, in observance of Jehovah's counsel to King Saul, they were allowed to take no spoil from their enemies.

Yes, it was a time of fulfillment—and it was a time of returning. All along the roads of the empire, Jewish warriors traveled to their homes from scenes of victorious battle. Having gone wherever the need was greatest, they had fought in town after town in every province across the map. In two short days they met the centuries-old command of their God to obliterate the Amalekites, and now they would celebrate.

Esther drew her lavender shawl across her shoulders and peered into the eastern sunset. Tonight, in Leah's village, as in all cities and villages of the empire, there would be great merry-making, and she would be with her family, for the first time since her abduction, to join the party.

She passed beneath the gate of the royal palace riding in a queenly carriage. This would be her last time to enjoy the luxury of such a conveyance, and the last day she would ever be called "Queen Esther." Granting her fondest request, Xerxes had agreed to return her to her people, once the "Day of the Jews," as he called it, had passed.

And such a time it was, of victory in war over the Israelites' foes. On the thirteenth and fourteenth of Adar the Jews of Susa were allowed to fight, and on the thirteenth the Jews of the smaller villages prevailed over their enemies.

Just this morning Esther had stood with her papa, Prime Minister Mordecai, upon the king's porch before all the people of Susa. There, together, they had proclaimed their blessing upon the ensuing holiday, enjoining all their brothers and sisters to remember the Hebrew glory from that generation forward in annual celebration of "Purim." For the dice, the purim, cast by wicked Haman to determine the date of the Jews' annihilation, had selected the very date on which Jehovah gave His people victory over their enemies and established them as citizens of the world.

Such happiness there would be in the old hometown tonight!

Hadassah, humble daughter of Abihail and beloved of Mordecai (whose name was now great in the earth), turned her dark eyes one last time toward the palace as it retreated behind the gated wall.

To her delight, Xerxes had stepped onto his chamber balcony, watching her departure with a sad smile.

Lifting a hand, she waved goodbye to him, and he, feeling many things, returned the gesture.

But then it seemed his gaze was caught away. And when Hadassah scanned the roadway, wondering what attracted him, she felt her heart leap to her throat.

Another noble carriage, this one heading toward the city, was just now passing hers on the highway. As it drew within the torchlight of the sunset wall, it favored Hadassah with a view of the interior.

There, barely concealed by a gauze curtain, was the unmistakable face of Vashti, a bit older than the girl remembered her, but beautiful as ever.

The returning queen was riveted by the sight of her beloved at his high balustrade. And her heart was full, it was clear, of love and forgiveness. In the king's embrace she would revel this night, and he in hers.

Vashti did not see Hadassah as she passed by. For this the younger woman was glad. She would rather not be known.

But if the lady had glimpsed the Jewess, she might have remembered the lovely child who had peered down on her from the garden rail so long ago. She would have seen the image of herself, and would have understood her husband's clumsy attempt to love another.

ESTHER

EPILOGUE

Better is the little of the righteous
  Than the abundance of many wicked.

The Lord knows the days of the blameless;
  And their inheritance will be forever.

Psalm 37:16,18 NASB

The lights of Leah's village square warmed the dark night as Hadassah wound her way through the merrymakers.

No one had yet recognized her as she passed through the dancing townsfolk and through the musicians who frolicked the night away.

She had slipped from her cab quietly, bidding sad goodbyes to Dorca and Maryam, who had ridden out with her. And she had privately entered the town gate.

She sought among the laughing villagers the faces of Leah and Moshe, and her cousins, Marta and Isha. But most especially she sought David. Her ears were atuned for his voice amidst the sounds of celebration, and her eyes focused for the hue of his hair and the angle of his chin.

But her cousins saw her before she identified anyone. And their squeals of delight drew the crowd's full attention to the newcomer.

Hadassah had always been a star to these folk. Since she was a child, she had captivated old and young alike. Now she was a regal celebrity.

No one had anticipated her homecoming. Vashti's resumption of the throne was news not yet delivered to the empire, and no one had looked for Queen Esther to be leaving the palace. That she should appear unannounced in this little place upon this festive occasion was a fantasy hardly credible.

As the reality of her presence dawned upon the locals, silence overcame the crowd, the music ceased, and awe marked every face. Leah, upheld by Moshe's strong arm, advanced toward the long-lost girl, tears spilling over her cheeks.

"My child!" she cried. "Can it be you?" the woman stammered, afraid to touch her, and bowing reverently before Her Majesty.

"Stand up, Cousin," the star smiled. "Call me not Esther. I am your Hadassah."

Leah turned hesitantly to Moshe, who could only shake his head. "We do not understand," he marveled.

"All in good time," Hadassah laughed, her dark eyes sparkling. "God's time is always perfect."

Nobody questioned her further, but Leah studied Hadassah's furtive glance about the square, and knew what occupied her heart.

"You seek David?" she guessed, drawing close.

"I do," was the simple answer.

The newcomer could see from her cousin's somber expression that all was not well.

"He went off days ago to fight at Ecbatana."

"Yes—yes," the girl replied, recalling how David had once spoken of the fabled city, and of the nomads who sang in the desert.

"We have not heard from him since," Moshe stepped in.

Hadassah's pulse quivered, as she feared to contemplate the meaning.

"Have others returned from that battle?" she spurred him. "Is David the only one missing?"

"Most have come back, but not our son," Leah sighed.

The younger Jewess hesitated, but then bravely insisted, "Of course not!" Then, trying to calm the quaver in her own voice, "He would have seen matters through to the end."

"We hope so . . ." Moshe agreed.

"How can you doubt?" Hadassah cried. "He is coming! He must come!"

With this she tore herself away from her friends, heading for the town's northern gate. Leah would have restrained her, but Moshe held his wife in check.

"Let the girl go," he soothed. "God is her strength."

* * *

Hadassah stood on tiptoe outside the low village wall, straining her vision up the highway which led to Ecbatana.

Overcome by memories, she trembled, gripping the rough slats of the gate and pulling herself as tall as she could stretch. How often she had done this very thing as she waited for David to come home from the fields! But tonight there were no homecoming workers to greet her, no friendly winks or nodding heads.

For long hours she stood, watching as darkness deepened, and as the villagers in the square danced and sang. She stood vigil until her legs ached and her eyes burned, and until the heat off the moonlit desert cast a shadowy mirage across her gaze.

Sometime past midnight her weary eyes were caught by a movement near a plot of palms which marked a bend in the highway.

Thinking perhaps she had dreamed it, she shook herself alert and focused on the spot. The more she concentrated, however, the more she was certain someone traveled toward her.

David, her soul pleaded.

But this man did not have David's walk. This man had a strange, limping gait—as one who had been . . . wounded.

Suddenly, as she absorbed the implication, she grew rigid. *Lord, could it be?* Before her intellect received the word, her heart knew. And when the moonlight reflected off his golden hair, she was charged with certainty.

Flying across the fields and the dry plateau beyond, she hastened after him.

The bone-tired soldier, the plowboy who had traded a hoe for a sword, fearfully studied the oncoming phantom. Something in the grace of the form was familiar, but not until he heard her call his name would he ever have dreamed it was Hadassah.

Even when she was upon him, flinging her slender arms about his neck, he could not accept what his eyes told him.

"My lady?" he marveled. "Are you a desert angel? Or have I passed on to Abraham's bosom?"

"Neither, my dear, dear David," she replied, laughing and crying at once. "It is I—your Hadassah. Like you, I have come home this night."

"Home?" he sighed. "To me?"

"Yes," she insisted, still clinging to him.

Suddenly he could bear no more, and thrusting her from him, he glared at her in torment.

"You mock me!" he groaned. "What have you to do any longer with a peasant?"

At this he staggered on toward the village, leaving her alone.

"You are hurt," she cried, seeing plainly now his bandaged leg and twisted foot. "Let me help you."

Rushing to his side, she pulled him closer, drawing one of his strong arms across her shoulders.

"Why have you left your palace, my queen?" he quipped. "Have you come out to play with the poor folk?"

"Enough, David," she returned, stopping still in her tracks. "You have not seen me for years. Is this how you greet me?"

The young veteran studied her quizzically, his pride more badly wounded than his leg.

"I will have a hero's welcome when I reach home," he said. "I need no greeting from the acropolis."

"And you shall have none," she answered. "I no longer live there."

The wounded warrior feared to contemplate her fevered eyes. Barely could he tolerate the hope her words instilled.

"Tell me no lies," he pleaded.

"Call me not your queen, then," she sighed, "unless I am queen of your heart. For I am no longer Queen of Persia. I am not Esther, but Hadassah. And I love you."

David's mind raced with questions.

"I am a poor man," he objected. "You have possessed a king's caress, you have owned an emperor's embrace . . ."

"I was his prisoner, David, not his lover."

"You have had everything . . ."

"Nothing—nothing without you," she insisted.

Tears quivered along the young man's lashes. The moon set fire in his golden eyes.

"Hadassah?" he whispered.

"Say you love me," she pleaded. "You have never said it."

Bending over her, he drew her to his bosom and breathed into her hair. His sigh said it all, and his lips met hers, to the soft sound of dancing beyond the village wall.

HARVEST HOUSE PUBLISHERS

For the Best in Inspirational Fiction

Lori Wick

Sophie's Heart

A PLACE CALLED HOME SERIES

A Place Called Home
A Song for Silas
The Long Road Home
A Gathering of Memories

THE CALIFORNIANS

Whatever Tomorrow Brings
As Time Goes By
Sean Donovan
Donovan's Daughter

THE KENSINGTON CHRONICLES

The Hawk and the Jewel
Wings of the Morning
Who Brings Forth the Wind
The Knight and the Dove

Lisa Samson

THE HIGHLANDERS

The Highlander and His Lady
The Legend of Robin Brodie
The Temptation of Aaron Campbell

Ellen Traylor

BIBLICAL NOVELS

Esther
Joseph
Moses
Joshua

MaryAnn Minatra
THE ALCOTT LEGACY
The Tapestry
The Masterpiece
The Heirloom

June Masters Bacher
PIONEER ROMANCE NOVELS
Series 1
Love Is a Gentle Stranger
Love's Silent Song
Diary of a Loving Heart
Love Leads Home
Love Follows the Heart

Series 2
Journey to Love
Dreams Beyond Tomorrow
Seasons of Love

Series 3
Love's Soft Whisper
Love's Beautiful Dream
When Hearts Awaken
Another Spring
Gently Love Beckons

HEARTLAND HERITAGE SERIES
No Time for Tears
Songs in the Whirlwind
Where Lies Our Hope

Ruth Livingston Hill
The South Wind Blew Softly

Dear Reader:

We would appreciate hearing from you regarding this Harvest House book. It will enable us to continue to give you the best in Christian publishing.

1. What most influenced you to purchase *Esther*?
   - [ ] Author
   - [ ] Subject matter
   - [ ] Back-cover copy
   - [ ] Recommendations
   - [ ] Cover/Title
   - [ ] _____

2. Where did you purchase this book?
   - [ ] Christian bookstore
   - [ ] General bookstore
   - [ ] Other
   - [ ] Grocery store
   - [ ] Department store

3. Your overall rating of this book:
   - [ ] Excellent [ ] Very good [ ] Good [ ] Fair [ ] Poor

4. How likely would you be to purchase other books by this author?
   - [ ] Very likely
   - [ ] Somewhat likely
   - [ ] Not very likely
   - [ ] Not at all

5. What types of books most interest you?
   (check all that apply)
   - [ ] Women's Books
   - [ ] Marriage Books
   - [ ] Current Issues
   - [ ] Christian Living
   - [ ] Bible Studies
   - [ ] Fiction
   - [ ] Biographies
   - [ ] Children's Books
   - [ ] Youth Books
   - [ ] Other _____

6. Please check the box next to your age group.
   - [ ] Under 18
   - [ ] 18-24
   - [ ] 25-34
   - [ ] 35-44
   - [ ] 45-54
   - [ ] 55 and over

Mail to: Editorial Director
Harvest House Publishers
1075 Arrowsmith
Eugene, OR 97402

Name _____

Address _____

City _____ State _____ Zip _____

**Thank you for helping us to help you
in future publications!**